EGGPLANT WIFE

EGGPLANT WIFE

J. Jill Robinson

J. JILL ROBINSON

ARSENAL PULP PRESS
Vancouver

EGGPLANT WIFE
Copyright © 1995 by J. Jill Robinson

All rights reserved. No part of this book may be reproduced in any part by any means without the written permission of the publisher, except by a reviewer, who may use brief excerpts in a review.

ARSENAL PULP PRESS
103-1014 Homer Street
Vancouver, B.C.
Canada v6b 2w9

The publisher gratefully acknowledges the assistance of the Canada Council and the Cultural Services Branch, B.C. Ministry of Small Business, Tourism and Culture.

Cover design and illustration by Kelly Brooks
Author photo by Shannon Brunner
Printed and bound in Canada by Kromar Printing

CANADIAN CATALOGUING IN PUBLICATION DATA:
Robinson, Jacqueline Jill, 1955-
  Eggplant wife

ISBN 1-55152-024-9

I. Title.
PS8585.O35166E3 1995   c813'.54   c95-910823-8
PR9199.3.R62E3 1995

Contents

Who Says Love Isn't Love? / 9

Acres of Affection / 27

Raising The Dead / 46

Eggplant Wife / 59

*This book is dedicated to two extraordinary people,
Steven Ross Smith and Barbara Scott.*

Thank-you to Jane Urquhart, Barbara Scott, Robert Kroetsch, Edna Alford, and Jack Hodgins (in order of appearance), for fine editorial advice. Thanks *especially* to Jane Baird Warren, whose critical acuity and tremendous generosity brought the collection to its final form.

Thank-you to the Sage Hill Writing Experience and the Banff Centre for providing me with fertile environments, and to John D. Fraser, the Canada Council, and the Alberta Foundation for the Arts for their support.

I am grateful for the existence of the fine cookbooks I consulted and consult on a regular basis: *The New York Times Sixty-Minute Gourmet* (Pierre Franey), *Chatelaine Cookbook*, *The Joy of Cooking*, *The Canadian Living Christmas Book*, and *The Gourmet Cookbook*.

Song lyrics in "Raising The Dead" are from songs by Iron Butterfly and The Doors.

"Raising The Dead" appeared in *Canadian Fiction Magazine*. "Who Says Love Isn't Love?" appeared in *The Fiddlehead*.

Who Says Love Isn't Love?

We drove out to Gladys and Lal's farm where Bess, of course, waited in the car. Must've got hot in there by three or so—there's no air-conditioning in the old black Ford, and in the house we were sweltering even in front of the fan. But Bessie can sit out there for hours on end, she always does, with her tin of Almond Roca and her bag of crocheting and her woman's magazine with its needlepoint patterns. You'd think she was an old lady. Someday, she explains if you ask her (if there's anyone left who hasn't asked her), she is going to learn needlework, and she has to find just the right thing to begin with. She sits there staring at those pictures for who knows how long, turning those curled pages. It'd take more than browsing through that one old magazine over and over again, if you ask me. But I wouldn't say that to her. Not on your life.

Why do you sit out there, I asked, exasperated.

Because I want to, she said.

Why do you want to? I said.

I don't have to justify my likes and dislikes to you, she said, all icicles and elocution. Now do I?

Nope, I said. Just curious.

Because I like to. That's all there is to it, she said. Promise.

I used to try to lure her out of the car when we went visiting. Nothing worked. Not a batch of new kittens. Not the smell of a saskatoon pie. Not the sight of the ice cream churn. Not me with my pants down and my dick sticking right out with wanting. You name it, it wouldn't work. I got sick of the game. Even got peeved for a while before I got it through my thick skull that what I felt didn't make a difference to what she did. But it troubles me every time. What a thing, when my own wife won't visit with my sister. Downright awkward when family won't get along.

She's just selfish, said my sister Gladys. Never thinks of you; only thinks of herself. She's always been like that.

Don't you talk that way about Bess, I said. But in private I do wonder sometimes.

People are welcome to go out to Bess, welcome to get into our old black Ford, but they've mostly stopped doing that. She's holding her goddamn court again, Gladys says. To heck with that. My kitchen or parlour not good enough, to heck with her. Let her rot.

Bess sees herself as some kind of enigma, Lal says, when really she's just a big pain in the you know where.

In the ass, says Gladys. Right in the big fat ass.

Well, I didn't want to say that, says Lal, with a giggle.

I'll say it for you. We can all see it, says Gladys, who isn't exactly tiny herself. It's not anything that isn't true.

Hey, you two, I said, indignant. It is *not* a big fat ass.

Depends on what you like, I suppose, brother dear, says Gladys.

Well what the hell else should it depend upon? Hm?

Rolling their eyes in tandem, the two of them say, Oh Clare. Have another cookie.

Eventually they got air conditioning out at the farmhouse, but Gladys and Lal didn't have even the idea of it that day. How to tell they're not your real farmers, but gentleman farmers, gentle*woman* farmers, I suppose is what you'd call them, although gentle ain't always the word for either one of them, particularly my sister Gladys. And not a hired man in sight. I suppose they might have a hired woman, if they could find one. Those two do everything, and I mean everything, public and private, by themselves. If you know what I mean. I'm not a one to go into details, you'll find.

So Bess was sitting out there in the car steaming like a Chinese pork bun. Some might call it stewing in her own juice. Could be that too. Dumplings in a chicken stew. One heck of a cook she is when she wants to be, but don't count on it. She has subscribed to this *Gourmet* magazine for as long as I've known her, but if you go and count on sampling those fancy recipes, or make the mistake of picking out a picture and saying How's about this one? and you'll be getting macaroni and cheese before you know it. Hold off on the comments and she'll gourmand you to bursting with Cornish hens in raspberry what's-it sauce and green beans armadillo like you never et in your life before. That's the way she is. Everything's got to be her idea even if it ain't. Makes for a somewhat precarious life sometimes, let me tell you. It's hard not to count on things when it's in your bottom nature to do so and you like a bit of security now and again. Makes me wonder how on God's green earth I ever allowed myself to get permanently tangled up with her. If I had a choice, that is. Which is another good question that's not likely to get answered.

I'll never forget the day—in Winnipeg, where I met her—that she took my two hands and placed them on her bosom. My face could've started a forest fire. One hand on each full, warm breast. I lost my balance and just about fell over when my knees buckled. Don't be such a chicken, she whispered, yanking me upwards by my wrists. Bock. Bock, she whispered, teasing. Chicky-chicky-bock-bock. Knead me, chook chook, she whispered. Knead me, you old rooster, you old cock, you old cocka-doodle-do. I do, I said, gasping for air and shaking like crazy. That's not what I mean, she whispered, thrusting harder against me.

Oh Bessie. Won't you please get out of that car?

So on this day I sat inside with Gladys and Lal—they offered me the parlour, I said the kitchen's just dandy—we'd fall down dead if we didn't have this exchange every visit—and into the kitchen we go, where Lal has covered up the Arborite table with a clean terry cloth. Big pink and purple flowers on the one for today, and a couple of cigarette burns right where you can't cover them up with a doily without it looking peculiar, from when Gladys used to smoke and drink simultaneously. Nowadays she won't touch either. And she's set the table for our tea. Lal's also not smoking today, I notice. The place smells different without it. Clean. Hopeful. Lal is getting a little paunchy, I see, but then hell, I've got a bit more around my middle now than I did when I was twenty, too. Bess, well when I met Bess she had a stomach hard as rock from pushing her old man around in that wheel chair day after day, and she's always been one for situps. Until recently, she'd tuck her toes up under the blue chesterfield in the bedroom and hoist herself up twenty, thirty times a day. With some things, she's like clockwork. With others, the mainspring is long gone and you can't hear a tick for love nor money.

There's always a tea cup and a bread and butter plate laid for Bess, though the last time she set foot inside the house is anybody's guess. It was Bess who pointed out to me about those cups. Me, I wouldn't notice unless I got no cup at all, and even then it might take me a minute or two. Bess told me that Lal chooses the cups real carefully, that you don't need to read tea leaves to know what that little woman's thinking of you. You can tell from the cup in a second. Don't ask me how she figured all that out, but something tells me it figures in why she sticks to the car now. Bess told me, you can rest easy if Lal gives you the one with the little purple violets. You can expect to take some chewing out and up if you see the one with the Egyptian design round the top get set in front of you. Plain ocher's a snub, and look out for the navy cup with the blood red trim and no flower. That's big trouble. That's mine, Bess said with a laugh. Tell her you want a different one then, I said. It doesn't work that way, said Bess. I don't know; I can't figure it out.

Lal and Gladys get ticked off about Bess's sitting in the car. Gladys did go out there once, and after a while we could hear her hollering through the glass of the window Bess had rolled up tight. Gladys was furious at being ignored. I thought she would bust the glass. I waved at her, said Bess on the way home, a little indignant. And smiled, sort of. I only started ignoring her when she wouldn't go away.

And today, Bess'll be interested to hear, everyone's cup is the same; it's their good china, with the garlands of fruit around the edges. Ain't Christmas, or Easter, or Thanksgiving. Everyone with the same cup, and the cream and sugar to match. What's this world coming to? And Christmas cake, even though it's mid-July, cut all nice and arranged so pretty on a serving plate that matches. I'm rattled by the sight, let me tell you. The layout reminds me of those tea parties people give after funerals. But I go along. Act calm, like there's nothing unusual. I'm wishing Bess was with me, I don't mind saying. Just to balance things a little. In the end I act the way I do with one of Bess's escapades. Wait and see but don't take your shoes off and be prepared to bolt, because this may be the best time you ever had, or the worst.

Gladys and Lal aren't exactly sisters, or cousins, though they're closer than most of the ones I've ever known. Haven't had one without the other since they started to play in the dust when our families lived next door to one another after my Dad came here looking for work and got some on the MacIntosh farm. Lal's family was working there too. Siamese twins, our mothers used to call the two little girls, though they hardly resembled each other. Have you seen the twins? one mother would call across the yard to the other. Where have those Siamese sisters got to? And then maybe someone would hear a giggle, and some little kitty mews, and out the two of them would crawl from someplace dusty and dirty, count on it. Here they are! Here they are!

Those two. They shared candies one of them had already sucked, licorice ropes, bottles of pop, you name it. Even gum one of them had already chewed—darn near made you gag to watch them pull the wet, gooey gob from one mouth and then stretch it into two pieces and pop the half of it into each of their mouths with their grubby fingers. And then off they'd go, grinning and chewing. Nothing ever belonged to just the one.

Funny, but sometimes they seem old, and other times they seem so young it's hard to believe. Easy as pie I can peg them as two old spinster ladies and next thing you know it's like they're eight years old, all surprised and thrilled with something silly. Come look, Gladys! Lal might call in from outside. Come see this ladybug! And Gladys will drop everything and go look, and the two of them will share the peering at this bug like it's the best thing that happened to them all day.

Gladys and Lal never really got a handle on Bessie, though to be fair, maybe no one could. And Lal and Gladys have been wrapped up in each other so tight from day one they've seldom had much use for anyone else their whole lives long anyhoodle. That isn't to say that they don't make time for family, don't make time for regular visits, and for helping out when they're needed. It's just that they prefer each other's company. And because Bess didn't come from around here—well that always makes a difference, doesn't it? Did I say I met Bessie in Winnipeg? The finest woman I ever set eyes on. I was a farm boy back then. Back then I didn't know how to act proper in the town right near us, let alone in a big city like Winnipeg. "Hick" is what Bessie's father called me, right off. What's a hick like you doing in town? he asked, leaning forward so's Bessie could light his cigarette. Buying hayseed? he asked. Then he tried to laugh and commenced into choking. I never had no use for that man, I'll admit.

Bessie and I have attended just two funerals together. The first was his. He passed on a few years ago now, but his passing was a gift from heaven, as far as I'm concerned. Gifts come in strange packages sometimes, but I recognized that one right off. Though Bess didn't.

The aide the old man hired after Bessie wouldn't give me up for him (though she still spent most of her time over there) had wheeled him down to the duck pond before she left for the day. Parked him facing the water, beside the picnic table. He had a little dish of pebbles in his lap—he liked to tease the ducks, fool them into believing he was feeding them, and he'd laugh and hack when they'd dive for the bits of what they thought was bread. The old bastard tipped over when he was reaching for his cigarettes on the picnic table and went face first into the muck and stayed there. The neighbour found him, Player's packet floating a little ways off, him all covered in mud and duckshit, wheelchair on its side. Who lugged him up to the house and cleaned him off a little before Bess got there I don't know. I never asked. Some things it's hard to care about. Some people are hard to care about when all they do is cause someone you care about endless grief. I knew right off Bessie would feel guilty about being with me—for not being there with the old man to pass him his goddamn cigarettes—until the day she died, even if I told her a million times what happened weren't her fault.

Bess is a gift, too, I've decided, though there's been plenty of times I'd have denied it. Gifts may not always be what you expect, or what you asked for, but who are you to say no thank-you? It seems to me that there might be big trouble if you turn a gift away. Take them as they come, even when they're dressed up more like Trouble at first. They can turn out to be the best damn thing in your life, and then your biggest fear starts to be that someone might take that gift away.

She bought a gold chain with her inheritance, and she

never takes that heavy bugger off. Spent everything he left her—which wasn't one whole hell of a lot—on that gold chain, and six pairs of socks for me. I told her I wasn't interested in anything that came from him, no offense intended, him being her father and all, but that I hadn't had much use for him when he was living, so it wouldn't be right to change my tune now. If I spent it *all* on just me I couldn't stand myself, she said when she handed me the six pairs of McGregor Happy Feet in six different colours. Now I can walk on that son-of-a-bitch *and* his grave, was the first thought that crossed my mind.

On this particular day it's news that Gladys and Lal are wanting to share.

You tell him, says Gladys, after pouring the tea. She is breaking a piece of Christmas cake into little bits. Making a little pile of the nuts on her plate. Popping the bits of red cherry into her mouth. It was your idea.

You, says Lal, trying to keep her hands steady enough to get her tea cup to her lips but spilling tea all over her hands and the tablecloth, onto the sugar she already spilt. You're better at telling. And he's your brother.

No, you.

Somebody cough up the info, I say, giving my older brother cough. Get a move on, girls. Haven't got all day.

We intend to get married, says Lal.

Married!

Well, that threw me for a loop, let me tell you. I mean, we all know their ... what do you call it, situation, but I thought we were dealing with it the best we could already—being polite, making no big public mind or notice of it, that's for sure. And they weren't exactly all huggy and kissy in broad daylight on the main street, and they didn't wear funny clothes and hairdos the way those ones in the cities do, the ones you see on the TV. What's the word I'm hunting? Bess would know. Discreet. That's it. They were discreet so's that no one who didn't know them would know, and no one who did had to. Most liked to think of Gladys and Lal as real close friends, a couple of unmarried, almost middle-aged ladies sharing a house, that's all. Unlucky in love, or the right fellas just hadn't come along. And some folks still thought of them as the twins. There was lots who still called them the twins, me included. And Bess, too, though she had other names for them as well.

And what is wrong with the current way of life? I ask, as calm and casual as I can. Just why do you feel the need for public display? I'm not sure it's wise, I say. For you two. Right now. These days.

We love each other.

Well, I know that. Anybody with half a brain knows that.

We love each other liked married folk love each other.

Well, I wouldn't know about that.

No, I expect you wouldn't, says Gladys looking me in the eye.

Lal nods, eyes cast down like some magazine blushing bride.

I'm not with Gladys because I couldn't get a man, says Lal in her small strong voice, her little hands all knotted together. But that's what people think. And I won't have them thinking like that if there's anything I can do about it. We're here because I love Gladys and Gladys loves me, and be damned anyone who says love isn't love unless there's opposites involved.

This time it's Gladys who nods, but her eyes look right at me. Be damned, she says.

Look, you two, I say, still trying to find the right position to take on this issue. People get married to have children. You're too old to have kids, even if you could figure out how to do it.

And you're getting too old for your own good, Clare, says Gladys, and Lal teehees in the background. You sound more like Daddy than you. "People get married to have children."

Like you and Bessie, I suppose? You're a fine one to talk about kids. You and Bessie have had a whole flock now, haven't you?

Touché, I say.

Leave him alone now, says Lal. Don't go too far.

And anyway, who's to say we're too old to have children, says Gladys, softer now. That just might be in our plans too, if you must know.

As you can see, Gladys can be a little starkers with the truth. But she did let several years pass before she asked why Bess and I weren't reproducing. I told her about Bessie's visits to the city, to the specialist, after her father died. The doctor couldn't find nothing physical wrong. Figured maybe something psychological. But worrying would only make things worse, she said. Trying too hard could cause trouble between Bess and me. Try to find fulfillment in some other way, she said. Those were the very words.

You must be forty! I say. Next thing you'll be telling me you want a veil and Kleenex pompoms on the car and a reception where you tink the glasses with your fork and kiss every two seconds.

So what if we do?

I want a wedding dress, offers Lal.

So do I, says Gladys. They exchange looks.

We want *two* wedding dresses, says Gladys, and they start into laughing as though it's the funniest thing on earth. Both of them have to put down their tea cups. The sides of my mouth start to twitch. The two of them all got up like they're playing dress up. I could picture that.

White?

That sends them into gales, and they carry me along with them. In a flash of sadness I wish for Bess. She should be in here with us.

Whatever goddamn colour we want, with or without sequins

and tassels and whatever the hell else we feel like having, says Lal, barely breathing, tears rolling down her face.

This is unlike Lal, I should say. She isn't usually such a laugher. Never has been. And she's never been much of a one for mouthing off, neither. When we were kids, she was the one squatted in the dust watching the ants walk by. Gladys was the one squashing them.

You going to invite the whole town? I ask, doubtful. I'd hate to have their feelings hurt, but I can imagine what some of the neighbours might say, guests or not. Not everyone's aware of proper guestly behaviour, not when there's a chance for gossip. And this'd be a doozy of an occasion.

This time Lal does the squashing. Let 'em come and gawk, let 'em stay away, makes no mind to us, she says. We'll be doing the neighbourly thing and asking them; they can do the un-neighbourly thing and decline the invite if they so choose. But our love, she says dramatically, won't be hidden no more.

And neither, adds Gladys, will our desire for a child.

Marriage? Children? What in the world had been going on around here? I stand up and go to the window. The car looks empty from here, though I know she's inside.

I sit back down, eat another piece of cake. If you don't mind my saying so, I offer, dusting cake crumbs off my hands and onto my plate, trying to stay calm, and act casual, there are some biological complications you need to consider before you attempt to have a child.

The two of them exchange a mischievous look and then Gladys says, We're already pregnant, if you really must know.

You might even say, smirks Lal and they both giggle, that we *have* to get married. It's going to be a shotgun wedding. You got one you could loan us?

I don't know whose belly to glance at. This is too much for me. I go back to the window. This time I can see Bessie's white hand. She's holding up her thermometer.

This is one of the many interesting and unusual things about my Bessie. She carries that blamed thermometer with her wherever she goes. When I go out to the car to drive home, she'll tell me, It was ninety-seven degrees in here! Ninety-seven, Clare! And when we go in our front door, she'll set it on the mail table, say hello to Banana, our dog, come back and tell me, It's seventy in here now, Clare. It was sixty-five when we went out. She has packed the thermometer around as long as I've known her.

When we went on the honeymoon I knew it was seventy-four in the bedroom, eighty-five by the pool and seventy-one in the restaurant. Our moonlight walk registered seventy-four. And three a.m. in our bedroom? Well. I tried to get her to rest the thermometer on her chest, but she wouldn't have none of it. You'll have to just guess how hot I am there, she said. And there. And there. About 180, I'd say, I whispered.

There we are, lying on our backs, sheers fluttering through the open French doors. Moonlight beaming. Us beaming. Thermometer rising. Me rising. What a night.

Oh Bess.

I suppose you each have a baby in your belly, too? I say.

You're getting personal now, Clare, says Lal. Watch your tongue.

But what's the *answer*? I say. Who's carrying the little critter?

Wait and see, winks Gladys.

Time will tell, says Lal.

They exchange one of those looks full of love. Downright shining, they are, like Bess and me on our honeymoon. You know, it never ceases to amaze me how one look at Lal can soften that granite face of Gladys's and make it look almost human.

You just give it a rest, brother dear, says Gladys, and kisses me.

All this real life family drama, and Bessie sitting out there with that tin of Almond Roca and a thermos of luke-warm tea and probably sweating to death with the windows rolled up tight and her wearing black like she's more and more prone to do these days, even in this heat of summer. Ladies don't sweat, Bess would say if she heard me say that. All right, then, Bess. You're out there *glowing* all over, from armpit to thigh to crotch. And thumbing through that same old magazine for the umpteenth time while at home are stacks of brand new magazines she hasn't even touched. Oh it's beyond me why she does that thumbing. Depresses me. I haven't told Lal and Gladys that Bess ain't feeling herself lately. Gets chills. Goes from hot to cold in no time at all.

Which reminds me of something. One August we had this fire at our place. That fire swept through our front hill and scared the bejesus out of us both and damn near took us and our house with it. What I'm getting at here is that that summer was followed by a brass monkey cold winter, and our house froze over. Froze solid while we were down at the coast visiting Marl and Byron. We came home to an ice palace, Bess called it, all the plants frozen solid and all the pipes burst, ice in the strangest shapes. Some like sculptures. The fish bowl, the fish, the shampoo, and bleach, and the strawberry liqueur in the liquor cabinet—you name it, it was froze. I built a big fire in the fireplace right off and that warmed things up in the living room. Bess sat in front of the fire on the hearth rug with a chopstick in one hand, the strawberry liqueur bottle in the other, digging out chunks of iced pink liquor like a bear digging ants from a log. All bundled up with the car rug, and stark naked underneath. That way I couldn't ask her to help me with anything, was my guess for why she'd stripped off in thirty-three below. How can I help you when I'm in my altogether? You want me to freeze to death? You do, don't you?

Oh yes. We know a thing or two about hot and cold, Bess and I do. In and out of her altogether.

Place and memory get stuck together sometimes, don't

they? One calls forth the other and they mix into a round piece of experience you can hold in your hand like a small bird, or a little ball of wool. Time gets all jumbled.

Gladys had an illegitimate child when she was seventeen. Now that was a jumbled time. Gladys and Lal broke up—the only time they had a serious quarrel, and it lasted almost a year. Over the stupidest thing, leastways in my opinion, and I'm not alone. The two of them were at the fall fair, and Gladys wanted to go up in the ferris wheel. Now Lal hates heights, and Gladys knows that better than I do. But something in her likes to try to make people do things they don't want to. Especially Lal. Nope, we're not going up in that, said Lal flatly. And Lal didn't want Gladys going up in it alone because she didn't want to be left on her own on the ground craning her neck to see Gladys sailing through the air in those big revolutions. But Gladys wanted to go, Gladys wanted to go. Kept hounding Lal, trying to ply her with cotton candy and hot dogs and more nickels for the digger machine, but Lal would have none of it. Nice, quiet, but No.

In the end, while Lal was visiting the ladies' room, Gladys walked up to two perfect strangers and asked if one of them would go up with her in the ferris wheel while the other one waited below with Lal. Lal was some mad when she came out and saw Gladys with those boys. Stood there burning while she was told what had been decided and arranged, and as soon as Gladys and the one fella were in the seat and the bar had been snapped into place in front of them and the fella had his arm across the back of the car, Lal took off. Went home, and wouldn't have nothing more to do with Gladys. Gladys stayed stubborn too, and ended up getting in thick with this fella—to irritate Lal further, is my best guess—and what happened next is as common as scarlet runner beans so it don't need expounding upon. She stayed at home while the baby grew inside her, and right next door Lal fooled around by herself and kept on going to high school. She got good grades, spending all that time alone with nothing much to do but study. There's a good side to everything if you can just figure out what it is. After the child was born it was put up for adoption and the afternoon of the day she signed the paper, Gladys and Lal were out walking together again, arm in arm, Gladys walking a little slow because of the stitches she had someplace female, and little Lal seeming to offer her support.

Well, goodbye, Gladys, Lal. Best of luck, and thanks for the tea.

I get in the car and unroll all the windows so's I can breathe a little. As we pull away, I say to Bess, Well, Gladys and Lal had some big news.

Oh? says Bess, putting down her magazine and stretching her legs out in front of her. I don't need to look in the rear view mirror to know what she's doing. She's putting away that magazine, sweeping crumbs off her lap, checking her thermometer one more time. Next she'll lean forward and rest her head on the back of the front seat. If she's missed me, she'll run a finger across the back of my neck and around my ear and I'll know what we'll be up to as soon as we get home.

Clare, guess what the temperature is?

I don't know what it is, Bessie, but listen to this. We're out of the driveway now, and heading down the road.

It's ninety-three in here, Clare. Or it was until you got in.

Bess. I got some news. But first I'm going to say right off, and I know you aren't going to like it, that you should have been in there to hear this. Those two are your family, like it or not, because they're my family, and what I'm going to tell you is family news. It pained me that you weren't in there to hear. Gladys is real important to me. You know that.

I hear you, Clare.

Now here's the news. Gladys and Lal are going to be married.

Married? says Bess, sitting forward just like I knew she would. I smile to myself.

Married? To whom? Clare? Whom to?

Each other, I say. Don't that beat all?

Doesn't that beat all.

That too, I say. And *that* ain't all.

Isn't.

One of them's got a bun in the oven.

A *what?*

Maybe both of them, for all I know. Knocked up. You know. Pregnant.

In the old days, Bess would be hitching up her dress and climbing into the front seat to hear me better. But she just leans more forward.

A *baby?* Which one of those dykes would sleep with a man, do you suppose?

My Bess may be feeling poorly these days, but she still has her tongue, by God.

They're not divulging that part. But Bess—how the hell would they have wangled it?

I can see Bess's face without even looking. That's one of the good parts about being with someone so long, getting to know them so well. Almost makes me want to pull over by the side of the road and watch her precious face as she turns the question over in her mind like it's a chunk of conglomerate rock.

Maybe a turkey baster. I've heard they use those. But whose?

Whose what? Turkey baster? For what?

Oh Clare. Dear. Sometimes you are so very dense.

And now her finger traces my collar, and I start to feel real good. I press down on the accelerator.

Well, I guess you want to know what happened in the end, don't you. You want to know was there a wedding, and so on. Well, yes there was. Some folks came, and some folks didn't, as could be expected. Gladys and Lal had to bring in a special preacher all the way from Vancouver, but he seemed a nice enough fella. And who was pregnant? Well, it *was* both of them, though the Lord only knows how they did it. They'll be having them any day now.

In the end, it was Bessie and our car that wore the white, not the two brides, in their magenta and their turquoise. In fact, I can picture the wedding as I sit here waiting on Bess—she wants me to take her into town, and I'm happy to oblige. She hasn't been too well lately.

Bess has me buy yards of white netting, and yards of white satin—and I can't figure out what the hell she's up to. The night before the wedding, she's up half the night—she decks our black car out in a big white hat, with netting over the whole goddamn thing like it's a face, and you have to lift this enormous veil to get inside. We drive at about five miles an hour, like we were a hearse, not part of a wedding party, all the way to the park, where the wedding is held. Bess gets me to pull right up close to the gate, near the garden. So's she can come in if she should so desire, I figure, hope springing eternal. But it's a pretty small trickle after all this time, let me tell you.

I leave her in the car, and join everybody else, and start doing my best man bit. We're about smack in the middle of the ceremony when out of the corner of my eye I see the car door open, and my heart leaps like a trout. Can't believe I'm right for once. Can't believe that miracles *do* happen. I'm the only one who sees, and I tell you, it's the happiest day of my life. I see Bessie get out, climb into Gladys and Lal's old station wagon, start it up, and drive out of the park. I see her take off the "Just Married" sign and put it on our car, and park it where the wagon was, for the newlyweds to get into when they leave the garden.

What a gal. Who'd dare to call her selfish now?

Then Bess damn near floats over to the high bank of

rhododendrons, the ones the colour of orange sherbet, and stands there, by herself. You'd think she'd chosen her lipstick especially, it goes so well with the flowers. And I can see how the heavy leaves cast shadows on her pretty face when she moves farther into the foliage and crouches down, in her white silk shift with its long slit up the side. That thick gold chain disappears between those satin breasts. She almost looks as though she's peeing, but she ain't; she's just resting.

 I'm still the only one who notices her. My Bessie's a knockout, and my eyes are drawn back to her again and again. I can see her now, in fact, as I sit here alone. In that bank of big orange blossoms and the big green leaves. I see her standing there until the service is over, and the confetti's flying, and then I see her motion, with her long sherbet fingers and lips, and her precious silken hips, for me to join her. And you can bet I oblige.

Acres of Affection

Barely after breakfast on Saturday, more than two hours before she expects Constance, a car turns into the driveway. Chandler doesn't pay it much attention; it's probably someone lost and turning around. But the car doesn't go; it pulls up near the front door. And then she realizes whose car it is. Sees the B.C. plates. Her parents; her mother is driving the Lincoln.

Chandler can see her mother, swathed in bright purple, and immediately her agitation rises. She fumbles the silver vase she is polishing. It falls on the floor and dents its rim. Damn. Around her mother's neck she sees a long chiffon scarf, its ends blowing out the window. Her mother honks grandly, pulls to a stop. Chandler's family emerges. Her mother with her pretence of crispness and efficiency. Walking straight from the car around to the front of the house. To check out something that isn't quite right, probably. Another slam. Constance has slipped like the weasel she is from the back seat. She buries her head in the trunk, then keeps her head turned away as she walks casually up to the house. Darn it, Connie.

Their father is the last one out of the car. He moves with unusual, surprising slowness. He walks alone and gradually to the bottom of the steps as though he is walking through water. He looks up at the steps as though they are insurmountable. Help him, you guys, Chandler hisses, drying her hands and moving quickly towards the door. It has been almost a year since she's seen him; what's happened?

He gestures away any help. I can manage, he says. He does not look well; his complexion is pasty. His hug is still strong, and his arms, hands, fingers are strong. As soon as they are inside, he says, I'd like to sit down.

Connie stands safely behind their father's chair, hands on his shoulders. Mum made me promise, Chan, she whispers, glancing around. She said she wanted to surprise you. She made me.

Chandler moves around beside her sister, out of their father's gaze. Creep, she mouths, and gives her a filthy look. Weasel. Connie smiles apologetically and pulls a cookie from her pocket. Sticks out her tongue and then offers Chandler the cookie. Chandler ignores her. Leans forward to kiss their father. I'm glad to see you, Dad.

Breathlessly their mother waltzes in, screen door smacking behind her. I *knew* there was something different when we drove in. I said so, didn't I, Gene? And I was right. There's a new trellis! A big new trellis. That Ryan. What you do to deserve him, Chandler Louise, I'll never know.

It's certainly a surprise to see you, Mum, Chandler says.

Well, we'd wait forever for an invitation, it seemed to me. And we haven't been out this way in three years. She removes her driving gloves and slaps them onto the table. Well, let's see. Your father would like his tea, she says. It's that time.

Constance reaches for the kettle.

Hop to, thinks Chandler. One two three four. The Great She has spoken.

How was the trip?

The roads were fine. We didn't get lost. We stayed with Constance last night. That apartment is far too small. Where's that man of yours, anyway? Ryan. Didn't you tell me once that he grew up here? Her voice drops to a whisper. I'd better be careful with what I say, then, hadn't I?

Depends what you're going to say, I suppose, says Chandler, remembering that they said this the last time, too. And the time before.

I can't imagine living in the place I grew up, her mother continues, and Chandler mouths the narrative in her head. I suppose many people would love the chance to live in my family's home, but not I. It must be different for a man. We really should get our things into the house, you girls. Do we know where we'll be sleeping? We'll be here for two nights. If that's all right with you?

You make the rules, Mother dear.

Oh come now. Your father makes the rules. I just have the ideas. I have a good one for this weekend. She pauses, looks from one daughter to the other in exasperation. Couldn't you two sit down at the table while I tell you? You girls never could sit still.

I already know your idea, says Constance, fidgeting.

Sit when your mother tells you, Connie, says Chandler, kissing her sister's cheek. Don't argue. Be a *good* girl.

Bug off, Chandler, says Constance, sitting down.

Their mother looks coldly from one of them to the other. Just what do you mean by *that* exchange? she says.

Where they live is a place in a storybook, visitors tell them. At least, the story books they used to read. Constance and Chandler are lucky lucky girls. Fortunate girls, and they shouldn't forget it. The side by side windows of their bedroom open out, onto garden. Chandler and Constance can look out to the rose arbour, grape arbour, cherry trees, lawn, and goldfish pond. To their log playhouse with the Dutch door, which is more suitable for playing pioneer woman than fine lady, though fine lady is what they inevitably want to play. Fine ladies get what they want. Fine ladies do what they want and boss people around and don't take no for an answer, though they give it all the time and expect to be believed.

At night Connie whispers honey sweet across the wide space between their canopy beds, Chan? You sing me to sleep, and then I'll sing you to sleep. Okay?
 Okay.
 Connie?
 Con?

Chandler tells the fan to oscillate, then turns her chaise longue towards the moving air, lies back, takes a bite from a shortbread holly wreath. Wipes the sweat from the back of her neck and between her breasts. She is waiting for her sister to come out. Her parents are wrapping Christmas presents in the den, have been in there for over an hour. Fifteen minutes ago her mother called Constance in. Shut the door firmly behind her, eyes barely glancing off her other daughter as she did so.

What Chandler herself is going to do for gifts is a good question. She sits up slowly, lays her head on her knees. Pictures roasting the turkey in this blazing heat. Mashing mounds of steaming potatoes in the sweltering kitchen, stirring boats of brown gravy. While outside, the world bakes. She sees her sister and herself, water dripping from their brows as one of them carves, spoons into the turkey's hot cavity to pull out hot, steamy dressing. After dinner the four members of her family sit on deck chairs, feeling stuffed and huge, unable to move, with big bowls of Christmas pudding hot in their laps, Christmas presents no one feels inspired to open under their feet.

The evening is still, and humid, without a trace of a breeze. Bloated and silent, the two sisters anticipate the piles of pots and casserole dishes that must face hot steamy water. Their father nods off and snores gently. Their mother sips a Tom Collins and tells them in sprightly detail about the challenges she faced on her shopping trip to find rubber insoles for her shoes three weeks ago.

Christmas in July is a stupid idea, as most of their mother's attempts at novelty are. But objection is futile. She has found all this Christmas stuff on sale, and by God she's going to put it to use.

Where will they sleep indeed. Another good question. Connie will have to help her drag the futon into the sewing room. Cram the tissue paper patterns, the cotton, felt, and fuzzy body parts for the never-to-be-stuffed rabbits, bears, and piggies, into the closet on top of the jeans, socks, and shirts that wait forever to be mended. The sheets of coloured beeswax and yards of wicking. What's Connie doing, anyway? Chandler closes her eyes. Lies back. There's nothing to do but wait.

Chandler squats in the creek with a mason jar, her head on her warm smooth knees. The brown minnows in the water bump their noses against her feet, then against the glass of the jar. She wants them to go inside. Eventually one will. And then another. She knows. She has spent many hours at this. She is good at this. All Chandler must be is still, and patient. She can be these things. Come on, little fishy, swim in.

She wishes she could be sick like Constance, but that doesn't happen often. And she wishes she could be good, but that never seems to happen either. It's as futile as wishing to be a different colour.

Mummy?

Not now, Chandler. Your sister has asthma. Out of the way, now. I have to fill the kettle.

Mummy?

Gene, her chest isn't loosening up. And that's such a dry wheeze. Should we call the doctor?

MUMMY?

Not now, I said! Go away! Get her out of here, Gene.

Go on now, Chandler. Be a good girl. You're in the way.

Nobody loves me. Chandler can see her own sad and serious face.

Her pixie cut and her striped t-shirt. Her small, thin body. Feel the yearning to be good and the compulsion to be bad. Remember how her clenched little body felt as she shouted I don't CARE. I WON'T care. You can't MAKE me. I won't I WON'T. I HATE YOU I HATE YOU WHY DO YOU HATE ME NOBODY LOVES ME.

Of course no one loves you, you nitwit, comes a scornful voice. You have to be nice to be loved. You have to deserve to be loved. Do what you're told.

Alone on her stomach on her bed, nose, head, plugged, heart aching and gushing pain, Chandler presses her doll's hard plastic face into her own.

How she would love to put her mother in Ryan's childhood room. With the flying insect collection shoved under the bed. With the stuffed barn swallows wrapped tenderly in cotton batting and tissue paper in the underwear drawer. Let her happen upon those. What do you suppose is in here? I'll just have a little look.

But her parents will have to sleep in the master bedroom. Chandler will take Ryan's room. Connie gets the futon. How will her Dad climb these stairs? Why hasn't anyone told her what's wrong? She opens the windows in the bedroom, props them up with a china shepherdess. Blows dead flies and spiders off the sills. Tips from great housekeepers. Dusts with her forearm, and with the bottom of her t-shirt. Dumps the contents of the top drawer of each dresser into the drawer below it.

When she comes back down, she hears her mother in the living room, sees her standing with an upturned candy dish in her hands. She is saying, This is Minton, for example. Minton is English, of course. I must say I'm a *little* surprised to find it here. So many people of—well—so many people are more inclined to have imitation. But some of the pieces here are quite lovely. And yet very few of them look familiar. She turns and speaks to her daughter. These aren't yours, are they, Chandler?

Who are you talking to?

Whom. I'm talking to *you*, can't you hear? I *said*, These aren't *yours*, are they, Chandler?

Of course not. I don't have anything nice. You know that.

Oh you do so, says Constance, coming in from the kitchen. That rocker is excellent.

Did we give you that? says their mother.

No, says Chandler. I bought it.

Is something wrong? Their mother straightens, while casting an icy eye on her younger daughter and letting it linger. Although, that is a dangerous question around you, isn't it? I should have learned years ago not to ask it. I must have rocks in my head. But here I've asked it, so I must be willing to accept the answer.

There's nothing wrong. With me.

And what about us? Their mother gives a short, false laugh and adds, We're not the kind of surprise you like?

Mum. Chandler lowers her voice to a whisper. What's wrong with Dad?

I can't hear you.

Yes you can. What's wrong with Dad?

I can't hear a word you're saying. She turns away, casting a baleful glance at Constance, who is eating a granola bar. Has she told something she shouldn't?

What do you know, Constance?

Nothing.

Did you girls get the bird into the fridge? And all the vegetables I brought? If they're not kept cold, they'll all be wilted by tomorrow.

Hello? comes from the kitchen. Is it time for tea?

Dad, you're out here all alone. I'm sorry.

I'm all right, dear.

Earl Grey or English breakfast? The only two I've got.

That will be fine.

Dad. Silly. You never change. I'm terrible. I didn't mean to desert you.

Oh no. I like a bit of quiet now and again.

Me too.

They smile at one another. Then her father says, I've been watching that bit of light—do you see that bit of light there? See how it just catches the corner of that glass and reflects it over there? That's quite lovely, isn't it?

Yes. I'm sure glad to see you, you know.

I'm glad to see you too.

These two sentences convey, she thinks, as she fills the kettle with cold water, the teapot with hot, acres of affection. They have always shared the same kind of humour, the same way of seeing. She feels shy about asking him about his health. It feels so personal. But she is about to try when the others come in.

Her mother bustles about with no clear purpose but to listen, Constance hovers on counter tops, leaves and returns as she follows her mother's curt instructions, eats a cookie, a nanaimo bar, a tart, carries in more things from the car—pillows, jackets, a plastic holly wreath. Their mother moves her eyes and her hands to everything, opening cupboards, drawers, closets, looking in, under, behind in constant peering, peeking motion. Isn't this cute, she says. Isn't this the cutest little cupboard. What's in here?

Chandler and her father sit at the table, exchange a wink.

Dad? Let's go out on the porch and sit on the swing.

Her mother stops in her tracks. Where are you two off to? To tell secrets?

No, Mum. Just to visit.

I like to visit too.

Mum—

Go on. I get the message. Loud and clear.

Chandler and her father sit quietly for a while, rocking

together. He takes her hand. She says, So how have you been, Dad?

Her father takes a minute to respond, then says with a sigh, Actually, I wish I were feeling better these days. I thought I'd feel like my old self a little sooner. I still tucker out faster than I used to.

What do you mean, a little sooner? Sooner than what?

Don't you know?

Know what?

I thought you knew. Connie knew. She sent me one of those big fancy get well cards. I had a little stroke, is what they say. A couple of months ago now. I was doing some tree trimming. Fell off the ladder.

Dad, why didn't anyone tell me?

I guess I don't know, dear. I did wonder at the time why you didn't send a card, but then I must have decided you were very busy.

A *card!* Dad, I would have come straight home.

Her mother is crouched down in front of the bedroom closet. The tails of her chiffon scarf drape down her back.

What are you doing, Mum?

Oh nothing much. She shifts uncomfortably, glances up. I think I dropped a button. My you have a lot of shoes. Imelda Marcos would be impressed.

Not quite. Chandler drops the sets of blue towels on the bed.

There are so many people in this world who never have even one decent pair of shoes. It makes me sad just to think about it.

Then don't. Chandler forces a smile.

Her mother raises her head with another of her looks, this one a combination: false amazement and displeasure. You'd better help me up, I think, she says. People weren't designed to stay very long in this position.

Chandler helps her up, and, once on her feet, her mother

pushes herself off like a boat from a dock and makes for the door.

Mum? I want to talk to you.

Well I was just going down to make myself a cup of coffee. Unless you'd like to make it for me.

Mum, what's happened to Dad? He isn't well.

Well? He's well enough, I think. I haven't noticed any huge or noteworthy change in him that I can recall. What do you mean? She pats her hair.

You know damn well what I mean. He had a stroke, and you didn't tell me.

Well, if you know all about it, why are you wasting my time asking me?

Why didn't you tell me?

I did.

No you didn't.

I must have. Surely.

You didn't. And you swore Constance to secrecy.

Now why would I do that? Maybe *he* asked me not to. I don't remember. She waves her hands dismissively. You just leave him alone. You are tiresome, Chandler, you know, with all your questions. You're not always polite about asking them, either. Sometimes you are downright nosy.

Why didn't you tell me about my father?

Her mother's face ossifies. Don't expect me to respond to rudeness.

The room is perfectly still for several seconds. Then her mother says, as she starts out the door, My, those curtains are quite awful, aren't they? Now, I daresay if I look hard enough I won't have too much trouble making myself some coffee. And then we are going into town. She sighs, looks heavenward. There's something not right about having to go through someone else's cupboards looking for things. Maybe Constance is down there. Constance? she calls in a shrill voice. She'll always give me a hand. Even before it's asked for. Constance? Are you down there, Constance?

I'll make you your coffee, Mum. Mum?

But her mother continues her monologue, overrides her daughter's words even as they're repeated, more loudly.

I'll do it, Mum. I'll make your coffee.

Her mother trails her dull, stale words out the door and down the hall to the stairs and Chandler's words squeak and trickle down behind them.

Chandler stands by the bedroom window with her back to the glass. She breathes in deeply, clenches her body as hard as she can. She tilts her head to the ceiling, crunches her eyes shut and emits the longest, deepest silent scream she is able. Her mind is fire; red, violet, purple, with licks of dark green, rage into black sky. She sustains the scream until her head is shaking and her lungs are empty and starting to heave.

Her mother is always mad at her. Sometimes she is In The Way, other times she is Impatient. With her bed, her arithmetic, her slip stitching. Why can't she be more like . . . guess who? Guess who, with her good girl attention and her sneezes and coughs. If, said their mother, she had called Chandler Patience, would she have grown into it? Her father laughed. Maybe nothing would help, he said.

But she is patient. No one notices. So what if Constance were called Chandler? What then?

Hi.

Thought you'd gone with them.

No.

Not go shopping with Mum? How can this be?

I said I had to help you.

I bet she was really impressed by that. I'm surprised she let you get away with it.

You still pissed off?

What do you think?

Brought some shortbread. Some homemade granola bars.

Constance, how dare you bring them here without telling me?

Mum made me promise. I swear. She would have killed me if I told you.

What about Dad's stroke? Fuck, you make me mad.

She made me promise that, too.

Why? How spineless are you, anyway?

Connie takes two more cookies out of the tin. Stuffs one whole in her mouth and talks through it. I don't know. I'm sorry. Really. I'm sorry, Chandler. I—

I'm his daughter too. Where do you two get off, anyway?

She said she'd pay my car insurance if I didn't tell you. I'm really really sorry.

Your car insurance. Well, that's pretty important.

I'm sorry. I said I'm sorry. Dad likes you. That's what it is.

He's *supposed* to like me. I'm his *daughter*.

I didn't say she was sane.

Well, she has *you*. Why can't she leave me alone?

Tears in her eyes, Constance holds out the tin. Chandler pauses, looks into her sister's unhappy face, finally takes a cookie. Sighs deeply before she bites into it, turns away. Then holds it between her teeth as she reaches into the refrigerator. Well, don't just stand there. Help me make drinks.

Look at me, Chan, Constance says, trying to charm, switching off the blender, pouring peach daiquiris into flutes. She slops some of the mixture on the counter, lowers her mouth to the edge, scoops with one hand while she sucks up the liquid.

Don't let Mummy catch you doing that, Chandler says.

Shit. Constance grins, her face flushed. Mum. Who cares? Chandler, look at me. In *general*, I mean. At my outside, and my sideways. She jumps off the stool, pirouettes quickly, shyly, and hops back up.

Kahlua cow, she says, aren't I? Did you see how my breasts and bum bounce? I'm sweet, creamy cocktails, aren't I? Grasshoppers. Brandy Alexanders. Once in a while a piña colada. Cha-cha-cha. Don't you think? If I were a drink?

I hadn't thought of you like that.

And you're white wine. Very dry. From Alsace. Hey. I know what I'd be if I were food, too. I'd be those little pastries that are way too rich to eat more than about three in one sitting. Petit fours. Wanted, but not all the time. And never for very long. But you think I'm a pie, don't you? A big thick banana cream pie. Don't you, Chandler?

No.

And you. What food are you? Connie's voice is getting an edge. She's on her third drink.

Here we go, thinks Chandler.

Maybe fresh spinach fettucini. With sun-dried tomato sauce. Something good, and interesting, and satisfying. Just like you. Right? Something better than just dessert. Good old predictable dessert.

I don't think you're a pie, Connie. I don't think you're just a dessert.

Then why, sister dear, are you in a good long-term relationship and I'm all by myself except for losers who last about a week?

That doesn't make sense, Connie. And things aren't always as great as you think they are here, either. Ryan's always gone working. Hey look. I don't want to be sun-dried tomato sauce. I'd rather be mushroom caps with tarragon and garlic. And a red and green pepper omelette. And icy cold grapefruit juice in a tall Swedish crystal glass.

That would work. Still unusual. Still colourful.

Why do you sound so angry? I'm the one who's pissed off around here.

It's just—nothing. I'm sorry. Hey. Maybe I'm peach cobbler with half-and-half cream. I'd eat myself right now. Two servings. Do you have any munchies?

Or strawberry rhubarb pie and espresso. You ready to switch to coffee yet, Connie?

No.

They're going to come back, you know.

I don't care, Chandler.

What's Dad?

Girl Guide cookies. Fig newtons. Milk. Scotch, water back, no ice. Strong tea and coffee. Your turn. Mum.

Chandler picks the petals from a flower. Hm.

Our mother. Our precious mother. Is medium sweet white wine from Kelowna. At room temperature. And purple grapes you think don't have seeds, but do. And stale water biscuits. At an outdoor patio on a cool day and you haven't got your sweater and you haven't eaten all day so your blood sugar is going wild and you know you'll have to sit there for two hours before you can escape to get warm and fed.

Oh God. Connie quickly looks around. Then she laughs. That's good, Chandler. That's really good.

They look at each other and then they both laugh, their laughter building until they both buckle over.

Wiping her eyes, holding her stomach, Chandler says, You kill me, Connie. You really do. So how are the kiddies at your daycare doing?

Still breathing. I think I hate them.

Oh?

And now Mum thinks I should move. Thinks I should give notice at the end of the month.

Are you going to?

I don't know.

Do you *want* to?

I don't even know that. Chandler, do you know how fucking—God that feels good—fucking tired I am of following other people's instructions for my life? You're lucky. You never had to.

Right.

She's always telling me what to do, and I do it. Why do I do it? Why do I keep doing it? You always could do whatever you felt like and nobody said anything except there she goes again. But if I did anything, look out. Connie's a *good* girl. *Connie* doesn't do things like that. *Connie* does this, *Connie* does that. Jesus. I don't even know what I want to do! Like the organ. Do you know that I never wanted to play the stupid organ? I hated that Mrs. Whitman. I hated playing. But they said I was good at it, so that's what I did.

I never knew you hated it, says Chandler. You must have been pretty good at faking it.

Connie sighs deeply. Drinks deeply. You know, the other day I went into my living room and just stood there and looked at it. At this big guilt-provoking thing, centre stage. Wished I had an axe. I'd sell it if I thought I could stand the guilt. I wish I *wanted* to sit down and play. But she wrecked it for me. I like listening to just about anything but organ music, you know. God. It would have been a fuck of a lot easier if I had loved playing.

And you. Look at you, Chandler. Look how happy you are. Real home, really nice man who would do anything for you. Security. And I can't even bring myself to play Christmas carols at Christmas. What have I got? Nothing.

Well, there's always Mum.

Thanks. You're trying to piss me off now, aren't you? Well it isn't fair for one second.

Ever notice how she hates us to be alone together?

Who? You and Dad? Yes, I've noticed.

But you and me, too. She always interferes. Interrupts. Needs you for something. You know what I think? She doesn't *want* us to like each other.

As she peels potatoes, Chandler pictures her sister, standing by herself at her CD player. Trying to decide what to play; worry and indecision, as always, mark her features. What is the *right* thing to do, to play, to say? Eventually, doubtful still, she puts on Brahms. Violin concertos. She's wearing a snug turquoise jump suit with a glitter treble clef on the back, and a couple of eighth notes on each lapel. Now Connie has a drink cupped in her hands; maybe a Spanish coffee. Yes. Chandler can see the bottle of Tia Maria, the mickey of brandy, the whipped cream in a can. The open jar of maraschino cherries and the sticky red juice that has dripped on the counter. Five or six cherry stems. Chandler can smell the strong Bolivian coffee. Can taste that first sip herself. Lick that cream from her top lip. Her sister decisively bites another cherry from its stem. And stares ruefully, angrily, at the organ, her face clenched in its perpetual look of worry. Has she ever been happy? She has never escaped.

Connie wipes crumbs from her mouth as she comes into the kitchen. Silently she takes the peeler from Chandler. Chandler slices dill pickles. Pours them both coffee.

Before you get started, says their mother, coming briskly in the door and pulling it shut, hard, behind her, Remember that your father won't go for anything elaborate. Don't bother with any of your fancy sauces and sauteed this and souffled that.

Just the straight goods is good enough for me, Connie says, imitating their father. She holds out an imaginary coffee mug. Waitress? Please?

Their mother holds the bread knife in mid-air. She says, Why are you doing that? What do you mean by that, Constance?

Nothing, says Constance, lowering her hand.

Well, it isn't very funny.

What isn't funny? Their father has opened the door. He stands on the sill.

Never mind, says Chandler, taking his jacket from him.

Tell me what's funny, dear. Just let me get a seat, though. I'm tuckered out.

His father was just like that too, you know, says their mother, taking her husband's jacket from Chandler and hanging it in the hall closet. Pats the chair where she wants him to sit.

Though your grandfather Baxter acted as though he'd get lost if he ever crossed the threshold of a kitchen. At least your father will come in.

Of course I'll come in. This is where all the action is. And all the women. He winks.

It wasn't entirely his fault, their mother continues. He and his brothers were all shooed out of the kitchen. Their mother brought them up like that. Dependent. You've never seen dependent like it. Couldn't make a cup of tea. I'm amazed your father can open the fridge door, though he seems to manage all right. Oh these men. What they put you through sometimes it's a wonder anyone gets along for more than five minutes.

What do you mean, "these men"? says Chandler. A swift kick in the ass and a half hour of hunger pains and most men would figure out how to make a cheese sandwich fast enough.

You are becoming more vulgar, Chandler.

Sorry.

Connie glances at Chandler over their mother's head. Winks. Chandler lifts one side of her lip in a growl. Touches the rolling pin.

Waitress? Could I get a little coffee here, please?

Dad, says Chandler. That's not funny.

What's not funny? I know it's not funny. My cup is completely empty. Not a drop in it.

Look, says Chandler. Why don't you guys just clear out and let me get dinner on, all right? Go for a walk or something.

We've just come back from a walk. I took your father

around to see the trellis Ryan put up for you. We're so sorry to miss seeing him. Now we're going to help. Don't you want our help?

Just go away. Please.

Chan, you just said you wanted me to—

I changed my mind.

Come on, Mum, says Constance. Show me your knitting.

Come on, Gene, says their mother. She wants us out of here.

For what we are about to receive

May the Lord make us truly thankful.

Christmas Dinner: Roast turkey with dressing made of white bread, celery, sage, salt, and pepper; gravy with diced giblets; canned cranberry jelly; steamed brussel sprouts; steamed carrots; boiled potatoes. And two bottles of wine. Dessert: canned pears, vanilla ice cream, chocolate sauce; cookies: chocolate chip, sugar, peanut butter, shortbread. And port.

Connie carries the cookies round, Chandler follows, trying to hold the coffee, cream, and sugar steady on a tray. She hadn't been able to resist a last glass of port in the kitchen.

Cookie? says Constance.

Don't talk with your mouth full, whispers Chandler behind her. Coffee, Mother dearest?

Their mother has a large cookie crumb on her upper lip that wobbles as she chews. Chandler forces herself to keep a straight face, though she desperately wants to laugh.

Say, will you have coffee, whispers Connie from behind her. You're not a tart in a truck stop.

Both sisters start to laugh, tremble. Two cookies slide off the plate onto the floor. Connie kicks them under the sofa. For later, she whispers, and they giggle again. Chandler can't hold the tray still, and can't put it down. Coffee spills and forms a hot brown puddle on the tray.

In my cup would be better, whispers Connie.

Yes, I would like some coffee, says their mother. In my cup, if you don't mind. Once you two have finished with whatever fit you are having now. Or you could share the joke with the rest of us.

Chandler is now laughing so hard she can't breathe. She sets the tray down on the floor and huddles there knotted with laughter. She feels the smelly black cape of her mother's disapproval descend on her shoulders. She waddles from the room beneath it, sound trapped rolling and turbulent inside, laughter turning to tears with each foot forward. Outside. Outside. Just get to the door. The door.

The air is cooling off. Chandler stands still, and straight, and breathes deeply. The almost chill air feels good against her flushed cheeks, feels good rushing down her hot, constricted throat. This silence is a gift. Her sister comes quietly out and stands beside her. They look upwards, outwards, into acres of starry sky.

Couldn't stand her another minute, Connie says, moving close, linking her arm through Chandler's.

Raising The Dead

For a month, the house next door stood vacant. Nothing could be better, thought Raisa. The guy who owned the house was clueless about picking tenants and she dreaded who he might come up with this time. There had been the ones with the two yappy little dogs and all the dog poop the people never picked up. And the ones who screamed at their three kids from seven in the morning until eleven at night. To wake up. To go to sleep. To smarten up. To stop crying. And there was the kids' response, too—always in shrieks and wails. Of frustration. Anger. Pain. Need. Finally those ones had been evicted for not paying rent. They kicked in walls and broke windows on their way out. The kids helped. She still thought she could hear them sometimes. The unpleasant ghosts of sounds gone. But usually there was just silence. Glorious, welcome silence.

The other houses around them, south, west, and east, housed elderly people who were always quiet, rarely outside. And when they did venture into the spring or early summer sunshine, they chatted quietly together, went on solitary walks up and down the block, gently stabbed a weed or two, turned the water on or off. Nothing major. Nothing even faintly disturbing. Raisa loved the neighbourhood. Except for that one rental property beside them. She prayed it would stay empty, burn down, get infested with termites. She'd been feeling practically calm lately. Or maybe the landlord would find some deaf people this time. That would be okay.

During the day, when she and Boney were home alone, the air and sound aligned in peace and emptiness, interrupted only by the brief, transient chatter of a squirrel, or a small bird's song, and she found her usual nervousness utterly quelled. In the early morning she worked on her writing—she was going to be an author of historical romances, if she could ever get started. Most often, though, she just wrote in her journal. It was getting fat after this past, tough year. Later she might sweep the floors, consider supper, play with Boney, weed twenty-five big weeds or forty small ones. Read, or chat a little, if any of the oldies were out of doors. Dump coffee grounds on the cat shit in the back of the garden where the corner stayed too dry. In the afternoon, at three-oh-five, she turned on the radio—low, very low—to listen to the pleasant voice and music of Jurgen Gothe. She had learned to turn it off at four, and five, during the news. She really didn't want to know.

Boney watched closely whatever she was doing. Boney lay, head on paws, and watched, eyes like an alligator's, turning, twitching, rarely blinking. Waiting for, hoping for, something edible in whatever she was doing. There seldom was, alas. Sometimes he fell asleep and lay so still she thought in a sudden panic that he might be dead. But a quick whistle, or whisper of the word "cookie," and he would jump up with a start.

Lying in bed each night, she and Luke talked quietly to each other before their words drifted into silence and they slept. It was the best part of the day, thought Raisa. The time she felt closest to him.

Luke?

Mm?

I love lying here with you.

Me too, Raisa.
Luke?
Mm.
Do you hear that? In the kitchen? The stupid tap is dripping.
I'll put in a new washer tomorrow. Or you can.
What about tonight?
No chancee. I'm beat.
Luke, please?
You know, Raisa, you'd be a great victim of water torture. You'd be whacko in no time. You'd spill the beans in a second. Where are your ear plugs? Didn't you get some ear plugs for on holidays?
I told you. I tried them before. I don't trust when I can't hear.
You can't sleep when you do hear. I know. You should go deaf, and then you wouldn't be able to hear anything at all. You could sleep as long and as hard as you want. You wouldn't have to listen to me, either, or the pots and pans banging in the stove drawer. You might become a permanently calm person! Let's do it!
Be quiet, Luke.
Why? I think it'd be perfect.
You know darn well that I'd get freaked out that I should be hearing things that I couldn't. I'd get neurotic. Okay, more neurotic. About bad guys breaking in. About sirens and windows and doors breaking.
And you couldn't hear Jurgen Gothe.
That's right. I couldn't hear Jurgen Gothe. What then? No music. I'd only want to be deaf part time, and that isn't possible. Just when it's dark, maybe. Or when our future neighbours make noise.
Deaf and dark. It'd be like being dead.
Her father's death, earlier this year, had been the worst experience of her life. She had never excelled at patience, or

passivity, but there was nothing else. To do. To say. Nothing. Something towards the end, in the final three months or so, made her want to listen, as she sat beside his bed. Listen hard. For what, she didn't know. But she felt instinctively, deeply, and strongly, that she had missed something as she sat there, as his death filled up her life, that she hadn't heard something that would have helped her cope, helped her understand, accept, bear. At his bedside she strained her ears until they rang, strained to hear not his words, for he was beyond words now, but something she was sure was coming from somewhere, some other dimension, maybe; perhaps, she thought, from the place of the music of the spheres, the place where the pure music stems, she thought, the music we can't hear but strive to emulate, recreate, record. Since then, since his death, and her first experience with an absolute—the absolute and permanent silence that death left in its wake—she caught herself cocking her ears, straining, straining to hear—something. At odd and unpredictable times of the day and night. Listen. Listen.

Luke?

Mm.

Are you sleeping?

No.

I want to tell you something. Something I did when I was little, when I was around ten.

A bedtime story?

Not exactly. No. Not a bedtime story. We had eight bantam chickens, and they ran around loose in our yard. They were really tame. They were my Dad's. He bought them special food, and called them to him when he fed them, and changed their water every day. One day when he was at work I grabbed his favourite banty hen by her feet, and then her neck, and carried her over to a two-foot stump. I laid her head down. She was squawking like crazy. Then, though I hadn't an axe, I pretended with one hand that this was it, this was just about it for you, old chicken. Say your prayers, I said. She became passive and quiet. As though she were waiting. But then at the last second I released her. I stroked her gently, and said everything was all right after all, not to worry. Then I put the chicken on the ground. She just stood there all dazed and ruffled, clucking steadily in a throaty sort of way, and then she took off. And I went for a second chicken. His second favourite. A black one named Cinders. Luke? Why do you suppose I did that?

What?

Pretended to the chickens that they were going to die. It's always bothered me.

Jesus, Raisa, that's pretty weird. I haven't the faintest. Kids do weird things. Don't worry about it.

I do worry. I can't help it.

Well, try not to. You worry all the time.

I know. I think of things constantly.

You've got to let go. I'm serious.

I know. So am I. She ran her hands across his chest, up the inside of his arms. His skin was so soft. Luke? Your skin feels old here.

How can it feel old? I'm not old.

It feels thinner, less strong and solid somehow than it used to. More like a kind of warm paper; as though it would rip easily.

Be quiet, Raisa. That's ghoulish.

She sat up and hugged herself. Oh God, Luke, just the *thought* of your getting sick and/or dying makes me lose my balance inside. If I were standing up, I'd keel over.

In spite of my aging skin and whatever else you dream up, I'm not intending to get sick or die just yet. Just make sure you keep me cuddled and warm and I'll last a good long time.

Raisa and Boney spend a Saturday hiking in Sundance Canyon, and when they get home, Luke says, Guess what. Our reprieve has ended. Our new neighbours have arrived. Your favourite: three guys. From a distance they look like old acid heads. Not much stuff.

Oh great, she replies. Do they have a big stereo? Big TV? Did you see when they moved in?

Big enough.

Oh I've Been Down So Goddamn Long
Boom Boom Boom Boom
That it Looks Like Up To Me
Boom Boom Boom Boom
Oh I've Been Down So Very Damn Long

Luke?

Mm.

I can't sleep. I hate those people next door.

You've never even seen them. Close your eyes.

My ears. I can't close my ears.

Try.

Their living room isn't ten feet from our bedroom. Luke? Will you please go ask them to be quiet?

It's just their house-warming party. It'll quiet down after tonight, I bet. Remember that song? The Doors, isn't it?

No. Luke—

Hush.

The next night it happens again.

There must be some way out of here
Said the joker to the thief
There's too much confusion
I can't get no relief

The windows vibrate. Boney whines.

Luke?

I remember that song, too, don't you, Raisa? Hendrix. "All Along The Watchtower."

Luke, it's even louder tonight. Will you *please* go?

No. You go, if it bugs you so much.

She takes the comforter off the bed and goes out to the back porch. On the south side of the house.

Move over, Boney.

Boney lifts his head from his bed. Lowers it with a groany growl.

Boney! Wake up!

Boney lifts his head again and yawns. Slowly rises.

Go sleep with Luke. Go find Luke. Good dog. You can sleep on the bed.

Better. She curls up on Boney's doggy smell. Starts thinking about hygiene and gets up to get a clean sheet. A pillow. Humanizes the bed, lies down and curls up. And tries to sleep, but worries, concerned about ticks, about fleas, about worms.

Lying there disturbed, tired, and alone in the silent dark, she conjures her favourite photograph of her father. He is seventy in the picture. He looks like a man Rockwell would like to paint. Kindly. Bright. Disease has not yet ravaged him. If she looks closely at his mouth, she can see the tip of his tongue, playful between his teeth. The next second, after the picture was taken, he stuck it out at her. It was his birthday, and he had no use for such milestones. You're as young as you feel, he said. Linear time? Diddly squat.

The next few days and nights are fine. The inhabitants of the house next door seem to be away, or calmed down; their metallic blue Trans Am is still parked in front, and there is a dark green pick-up truck with a camper out back, but Raisa sees no one coming or going during the day, and at night the house is dark. There are lights on in the garage, however, but very little sound, all night long. Maybe they are mechanics, she thinks.

Nocturnal mechanics? says Luke. Maybe they dismantle or repaint stolen cars.

But they don't make enough noise for that. She still has never actually seen these guys yet. Just their shadowy outlines in the night and behind the blinds, and their sounds. But then, they don't keep the same hours.

While things stay quiet, she stays in the bed in the bedroom with Luke. Boney goes back to his. I'm glad about this, says Luke. But then,

Innagadadavida, baby
Don't you know that I LOVE you

She stands in the doorway to the bedroom, candle in her hand.

Luke?

Iron Butterfly. God, Raisa, you scared me. You could be the Virgin Mary standing there like that. Or Santa Lucia.

Look. I don't think I'm being difficult. All I want is quiet neighbours and I have the right to peace and quiet, damn it. You are zero support and zero help, Luke. I'm going to sleep in the basement.

Why?

So it'll be *quiet*. So I can't *hear* what I don't want to *hear*. I won't be able to hear them down there, will I?

Probably not. But Raisa—

Down the cold steps to the basement. Past the washer and dryer, past the night light with its feeble, perpetual glow. Like entering the mine in Sudbury. Down into dark wetness. Hear the water dripping dripping wetly into invisible puddles. Not quite so wet here. Around and into the Little Room. The little, cold, concrete room, never finished, just barely roughed in. Wooden shelves for canning she hasn't done. Boxes. Potting soil. Big plastic bags containing big soft lumps. A dirty old curtain for a door. Concrete floor glued with indoor-outdoor carpet. She stops, holds her breath, listens. Nothing. Nothing but the hum of the hot water tank. Great. Hiking pad, sleeping bag, pillow, watch. Flashlight.

Boney. Come on.
Boney. *Now*. Come.

She lies on her side in her sleeping bag and listens. Nothing. Sweet, sweet silence.

Boney lies mournful and unimpressed beside her. He hates the basement. She kisses him, scratches his tummy.

Good night, Boney dear.

Down here when she pictures, through no choice of her own, she sees her father in his coffin, the day before the funeral. She had not wanted to see him dead this way, this post mortician way. It was her mother's demand, an old country custom. They can fix him right up, her mother insisted. They can fix him right up. No, Mum. No. Don't do it.

He was so thin. So very, very thin. They must have poked stuffing under his lips, behind his cheeks, even pumped some into his hands; then they rouged and powdered him 'like some goddamn dandy'—is how he would have put it. Lying in her sleeping bag Raisa saw the picture as though she were floating above the scene; below, she saw herself standing beside him, trying so hard to hear, while his body, in sickening parody of life, lay ready for the rituals.

One day maybe two months before the end, he had whispered to her, I want to see myself. Let me see my old carcass one last time.

Oh Dad. No you don't. You'll get vain.

Bring me a hand mirror, would you dear?

She'd had to go buy one. When she got home, she took the 5x7 photo from its frame and taped it in.

Here you are, Dad. The real you.

That bad, eh? he said. Dear, he said. I want to see myself as I am. Please.

Slowly, reluctantly, she picked off the tape. Eased the picture out. Put the mirror on his stomach, faced down.

Now leave me alone for a few minutes, would you? Thankyou. When she returned, her father was sleeping, his hands clenched together on his chest. The mirror was on the floor.

It is so cold down here, she thought, pulling Boney close, worming her way deep inside her sleeping bag. So very very cold.

In the morning the outside of her sleeping bag is damp.

Boney is shivering slightly, tight up against her. Dim light permeates the window. Upstairs the light is pouring in through the windows, she knows, and it is warm, and Luke is stirring. We are in prison, she thinks. We are in prison, my dog and I, and all of the outside world we're ever going to see is through that crummy, dirty little window. Eventually Boney will get old and die, and then I'll be totally alone. His bones will lie right there in the corner because I'll be unable to bury him, and every day I will look at them and wish I could pat him again, wish I could kiss the bridge of his nose again, and I won't be able to. Ever again. I'll be locked in here forever, with arthritis from the damp, and I will write my historical romance novel on the walls, if I can find a pen and hold it in my gnarled hands long enough. Who will bring me gruel? Who will bring me a bed pan? Who will bring me coffee in the morning?

Luke?

Luke?

Squeak squeak above her he crosses the kitchen floor. He will push the button on the coffee maker before he goes to shower. But he won't bring the coffee down. He hates basements too. Boney stands whining at the door. He wants to go outside.

Forgot about that, Boney. Sorry. She opens the door and he shoves it wide open with his nose and races up the stairs to his dog door.

So much for solidarity, dog, she yells up behind him.

Luke doesn't ask her how she slept.

For several nights she lies in her basement bed. Boney her reluctant companion. I'm dead; Luke said it's like being dead, she thinks. Inside my head, dead space and air, and my hungry thoughts. Big slabs of wet rock. Gigantic building blocks of stone dragged by hundreds of slaves to build the impermeable wall around my ears. And nothing, nothing will move the wall away again until the light returns, save for the kind of explosion that would easily finish me off in the process. K*aboom*. The end. Alone.

Luke? Will you come and sleep with me?

Down in that cold basement when we have a perfectly good and comfortable warm bed right here?

Yes.

No.

Please?

Raisa—

For five nights they descend to the cellar together. Before they fall asleep on the fifth night, they hear the muffled ring of the phone in the kitchen above them. Seven times. Eight. Nine. It is late. The ring sounds very far away, up in heaven, maybe.

Who was that?

Who knows? They'll call back. I'm freezing, Raisa. I'm going to freeze to death down here and then you'll be sorry. But you can buy a lot of insulation for a hundred thousand dollars, so maybe you'll be all right.

You're not going to die. At least, not right now.

Raisa? Remember your killing the chicken story?

What about it.

Maybe it's about not being able to have control over everything. These guys next door are another example. And even if they move away or drop dead there'll be something else. Something's always going to wreck your quiet. So you might as well just get used to it. Things don't always work out the way you want them to.

Sometimes they do, if you want them to badly enough. If you try hard enough.

The morning is unbelievably still. There is dew on the grass, and the grass itself seems particularly green, the sky especially blue. The colours in her garden—the purple of the delphiniums, yellow of the buttercups, pink of the wild roses—are unusually vivid. How alive everything seems. An omen, she thinks. An omen for better times. Travel hopefully, her father always said. Travel hopefully or there is no point in the travel.

Luke stands breathless at the door.

Guess what? That was their landlord on the phone last night. Those guys were drug dealers. They skipped out. He wanted to know if we'd heard anything. I just went over there. The garage smells like a pot factory. They were just getting stuff set up and something must have scared them off. Gone in the night like thieves.

And took their noise with them.

They did.

Will you help me move my stuff back upstairs?

Boney, Lie down.

Boney lies down.

Play dead, Boney.

Boney rolls over onto his side, flops his head out flat.

Now stay. Stay, Boney.

Boney lies still as she decorates him with tissue paper flowers—turquoise, green, purple. As she tucks blossoms all the way around his brown pudgy body, on his paws, over his ears, on the bridge of his nose. Stay.

Sprinkles him—and the tissue paper flowers—with rose water from a pretty jar with holes punched in its lid, all the while moaning, moaning low in a kind of a chant.

There he remains.

She stops and stands over him.

Here lies Boney, good good dog, she intones with forced solemnity and a rumpled brow. Here lies Boney, best dog in the world. Boney was such a good dog, she says, sadly now. What a good dog who can't eat *cookies* any more. Boney's tail twitches, flips, ever so slightly. Paper flowers rustle. Release and cookies are imminent.

Luke watches from a distance, from the side, the corner

of the house. She has the dog on a white bedspread this time, folded into four like some kind of tasseled mat. Who would carry the corners? Not he.

Okay! Good Dead! Good Dead, Boney! she cries, and up he springs. Up springs Boney to tear around the yard in a wild, sure circle of dog glee, of which she is the centre. Around and around at full throttle and ever so much alive. A bark or two for exclamation. I live! I'm a damn good dog and I live! Flowers everywhere. Trampled. Tossed. Muddy feet on the burial mat. A gleam in his eye. And she? Clapping, clapping as he runs by, clapping and egging him on, around and around.

Eggplant Wife

DECEMBER

Mitch? Lucie hops up and down in the cold. Have you got your key?

Yes. Slowly he takes off his sheepskin gloves, hands them to her, searches his ski jacket pockets, then his jeans. Holds out the key on a rabbit's foot.

She looks down at the furry pink paw, and then up at his face, obscured by his scarf.

Well, let's go in, she says.

Lucie, I can't, comes his voice through the wool. I don't want them not to be there.

Mitchell. Dear one. You have to go in. It's freezing. Here. Give it to me.

Gingerly she takes the rabbit foot from him and inserts the key in the door. And enters first. He stands behind her, tall and unhappy in the open doorway. Hot air, fogging up like mist behind him, billows as it hits the intense cold beyond.

Leave things as you'd like to find them. Somebody's motto. Battered linoleum gleaming from a recent waxing and buffing. Winter work boots lined up by a big wood stove, though it isn't the only stove—there's a gas one as well, over by the big white refrigerator. The scarred and chipped Arborite counters have been bleached so often the original red is scuffed with a milky sheen. How much dough has been rolled out on that counter? Lucie wonders. How many loaves of bread cooled and sliced? Nothing in the kitchen sink but a rust spot from the dripping tap. On the window sill behind it, a frog that holds a scrubber in its mouth, and three dusty ceramic vegetables in a green wicker basket—a bunch of young carrots, a green cabbage, a dark purple eggplant. She reaches to pick up the carrots; walks over and they fall apart—they've been broken and placed back without being mended. The cabbage and eggplant are both whole, however. The cabbage has bad chips on a side turned away to face under, but the eggplant is certainly worth saving.

Walking in here is like walking into their lives. Mitch's mother's apron is on a hook beside the door to the living room, his father's cardigan rests on the back of a kitchen chair. Mitch puts his hands on the burgundy wool as though on a shoulder, then turns to Lucie, jaw clenched so tight, cheek pulsing so hard, she can hardly understand what he is saying.

Christ, Luce. They've got to come home.

Her confidence collapses. She feels small, inadequate. How can she offer anywhere near enough comfort to him? She goes over to him, holds him from the back, arms around his middle. She hugs him tightly as she can.

Oh Mitch, she says. He doesn't respond. She wishes he would turn to her, lower his curly black-haired head onto hers as he normally would. She has always been able to soothe him. He remains feeling brittle and cold; his surface is enough to give her goose bumps, inside and out. But she stays with him, holds him, her head against his stiff, hard back.

Her mind skips involuntarily ahead. To stoking that wood stove. To dusting under the lime green doilies she can see through the doorway into the living room—wouldn't her parents have something to say about those! Well, her father, anyway. To the horrendous amount of painful work in store in the not too distant future. Emptying the closets, the underwear drawers. Happening upon secrets tucked away. She can hear the sound of shoes being thrown in a big cardboard box, and the hollow thuds make her shiver. Everything into boxes and then these boxes lugged out and stacked on the front porch. The emptiness death brings, echoing certainly through this house.

This is a peculiar way finally to meet them. By embracing not them, but their home. Mitchell wouldn't let her meet them before; said they would be troubled by their not being married, though she has always suspected there is more to it than that. For all she knows, they didn't know she existed. This Easter that was to have changed. This Easter. Doesn't matter now.

The night they received the news, they lay in bed together and he stroked her. Stroked her with his big, soft hands, up one long leg and down the other, then up along waist, ribcage, breast, to shoulder and down again, pausing at the curve of her hip. As though he thought he could soothe his deeper pain by soothing a surface. He said then that his father was a quiet man, and that his mother could, sometimes, be a little hard to please, but was nevertheless a good, good woman who loved her family—him, his father—dearly.

Their trip to Hawaii had been a present from Mitchell, a surprise. They hadn't taken a holiday for years, and took it only because he gave it to them.

They go because of me, and look what happens, he said, pushing his fingertips gently but firmly into her hip, pushing her flesh against her bone. He was trying, she imagined, to express anguish through touch. While she remained almost silent, unable to find appropriate words. Words that could help at all.

Hush, love, she said, kissing him, moving closer to him. How could you know this would happen?

And what did I ever do for them? Left them. Wouldn't stay on the farm. What a selfish prick.

Hush, love. You're not.

Lucie. What would I do without you?

He's as far from selfish as she can imagine. He's gentle, and good, and far too sensitive. Once he found an injured robin on their apartment patio, and instead of leaving it there for the cold or a cat to get, he put it in a shoe box lined with cotton batting. Then he carried it out to his truck, and started the engine. He folded that long, long body down onto the ground, and crouched there holding that box, cooing at that bird under the exhaust fumes until the bird slept and died. Then he buried it; even made a little cross.

Later, on the night of the call, he woke her up. Lucie, he said, twining shanks of her hair into long ropy tendrils. I have to go home.

Home? To Alberta? Why?

Lucie? Will you come with me?

She took her hair from his hands. Unwound it slowly.

Why do you want to go? What do you think you can do?

If they come back, we'll be a great surprise for Christmas.

She stared into the darkness, then up, at the fluorescent stars sprinkled across their bedroom ceiling.

And if they don't, Mitch?

Well, then at least the place will be looked after properly. It's the least I can do, don't you think? You'll love it there, Luce.

But we'll miss Christmas.

No. We'll have it in Alberta.

Mitch, I've never been away from my family at Christmas.

Lucie, I have to go.

This is what he needs. To go. To his parents' empty farm house. To face, through seeing their absence, the fact of their certain death. This, the last thing on earth she wants to do right now, near Christmas, leave her family, her home. Go willingly to the cold and foreign.

Okay. We'll go. For a while.

You're great, Lucie.

I've never been on a farm.

You'll love it, Lucie. I know you will. And he kissed her warmly, fully, the nub of his beard grazing her slightly. Come here, he said, pulling her close.

I'm not pleased about your going off to Alberta, said Lucie's father, pouring two fat fingers of scotch from the leather-bound decanter. And I'm not going to pretend for one second I am, just to make you feel better. Listen up to your old man. I didn't raise you to wind up with a bumpkin.

Dad, Mitchell is not a bumpkin.

So you say. Here. Her father took out his cheque book. You're going to need something to tide you over while you're out there stubble-jumping. Haven't you heard? It's as easy to fall in love with a rich man as a poor man.

Dad—

And what the hell is your mother supposed to do without her little girl on Christmas? Come to think of it, what are *you* going to do on Christmas? String popcorn and cranberries? Pluck your own goddamn turkey?

Mum and Les will be here with you.

Lucky me. A fruitcake and a fairy. He laughed.

Mel, stop it, said Lucie's mother. She feels she needs to go.

Don't you Mel me. Lucie, you tell what's his name to go if he wants. I want you home for Christmas. You don't even know these people.

I have to, Dad.

And what about us? What about your brother? Your mother? Nancy, you talk to her.

Her mother, looking down, pulled leaves from a flower arrangement sent for their anniversary, long dead. She's made up her mind, Mel. We'll have to accept that.

Maybe you do, but I don't. Get me some ice.

Oh Dad.

Now a lean tower of sadness in his parents' kitchen, Mitchell turns to face her. Come here, okay? he says. They slowly climb the stairs, holding hands, and he leads her to his boyhood bedroom. There is a race car bedspread on the bed, and matching sheets and pillow cases. There are model airplanes suspended from the blue ceiling on lengths of fishing line. As though, Lucie thinks, he left home when he was thirteen, not twenty. The room is icy cold. They make love, with the door closed. There is an urgency in the way he takes hold of her, clutches her, as though she isn't herself, but a thing, a way to make something happen. He keeps saying Sh, Sh, as though his mother and father were outside the door, or across the hall in their bedroom, or below them in the kitchen.

Mitchell, no one's here, she says, shivering. There's no one here but us, Mitchell.

Sh. Shhhhh.

Their lovemaking is intense. Abrupt. Afterwards he turns from her to lie on his stomach. She rubs his back slowly, feels him tremble, then break into sobs. She pulls the covers up over them.

Could you give me some time, do you think? His muffled voice comes heavily from the thick white feather pillow.

Sure, she says, uncertain of what he means.

One, two. Down. Down. Rip tides and the swoosh, swoosh of waves, on and on and on. The disappearance of Mitchell's parents was witnessed by one man only. One man who confessed he was ripped—higher than a hawk's nest is what he said—on some pretty wild Hawaiian pot and not really paying any attention when these two quite ordinary and late-middle-aged people walked into his vision's scope and after a while were gone. But he didn't report their disappearance; he wasn't absolutely sure that they were there in the first place. It was like trying to decide, he said later, if you'd seen a particular sea gull, or some ordinary motion of the waves. This is Hawaii, man, he said. Imagine me going to the cops and saying

I saw a couple of tourists on the beach and then I didn't see them on the beach. This is Hawaii, man.

It's a small family farm near Dahlia, Alberta; a tiny village half an hour from Calgary. Gas station, grocery store/post office, a few houses and other small farms. On the farm, the house, a barn, and three smallish outbuildings. All under snow. And a fat unruly dalmatian named Spot, retrieved from the neighbours, who likes to trail after her, panting.

Until Lucie and Mitchell arrived, the house sat tall and white and empty, waiting patiently for its owners' return. Until Mitchell and Lucie backed away from their Vancouver apartment building, turned their backs on the evergreen wetness of her home landscape and drove away, up the long valley into the mountains. When they emerged again it was into increasing flatness, brown, white, and cold. Into a city and out of a city, to the outskirts of Dahlia. Then up the long, gravel drive.

The inside and outside lights on the farm—including the barn—have been rigged up to go on and off with an elaborately co-ordinated system of timers which ended, finally, with one master plug near the kitchen door. Mitchell's father set up and installed each timer before he and his wife went on holiday. The yard light, bathroom, living room, hall, and bedroom lights are all co-ordinated so that if you sat for a twenty-four hour period you could probably imagine a day in their lives.

Might as well shut all this stuff off now, Lucie said, reaching to pull the plug.

No! cried Mitchell, and roughly he took the plug from her hand and reinserted it in the wall. Leave it alone, he said gruffly, then added, more softly, after seeing her expression, How about.

It's your house, she said quietly. But that was a little rude, you know.

I'm sorry, he said, and left the room.

If you wanted to, thought Lucie, you could almost imagine that a kind of a charm were being worked here. You could even imagine how a person could convince himself that by keeping the imitation of motions established, he could ensure that the people would return to slip into those motions.

She feels like a usurper the first time she cooks in the pale orange kitchen. She doesn't want to cook at all, but that can't continue indefinitely. And she knows she'd better at least try out the stoves, try to figure out where everything is, before she attempts an entire Christmas dinner. They did a lot of take-out at home, they were both so busy. Now, she said to herself in the hall mirror, you can try your hand at being a real *wife*. Then she adds in a whisper, Just like Mitchell's mother. And raises her eyebrows at her reflection.

Lucie sits at the rickety kitchen table and leafs through his mother's cookbooks, hoping to find favourite recipes that will surprise and please him, cheer him up. She feels as though she's being watched the whole time; as she selects a knife from his mother's set, opens his mother's canisters, hunts through his mother's cupboards.

Lucie's been watching Mitchell out the window. Watching him tramp around and around the yard as though he were casting a different spell, around each building, looking up, looking down, touching corners, checking doors, going into each building and coming out again, then repeating the whole process. Seemingly passive, seemingly pointless. He is wearing a red and black flannel jacket and hat she has never seen before, an outfit that transforms him instantly into her stereotype picture of farmer.

At twelve on the nose he comes back to the house, stamps the snow off his feet. When he takes off the cap, his thick black hair is a static-filled, unruly tangle. His cheeks are almost ruddy.

Well, you look right at home, she says with a smile. I half-expected to see a milk pail in each hand.

This isn't a dairy farm, Lucie, he says with a quick sharp smile. You really are from the city, aren't you? Brrr Nellie it's a brisk one out there. Got some coffee on for the old man?

Old man? she says. Is that what you are, my love? My old man? But I'm not a farmer's wife, she objects, slightly embarrassed. I'm one of those painted, no good city women, living in sin. Remember me? She draws a tea towel seductively over her shoulder.

Mitchell gives her another small smile. He takes off his jacket and hangs it up on the hooks by the door in one smooth, familiar motion that ends with his sitting at the kitchen table.

Soup smells good, he says, rubbing his hands together.

Your Mum made it.

He looks at her sharply.

I'm sorry, Mitch. I just—I found it in the freezer downstairs. Buns, too.

Oh.

They smell really good, don't they? Did you want to eat in here, or in the dining room? Mitch?

May as well eat in here. No point getting fancy.

Sure.

He gobbles his soup and bread, drains a mug of coffee, stands and stamps for no reason she can see, and goes back to his coat and boots.

Where are you going? she says. You're always *doing* something. Sit down and have coffee with me. Aren't we on holidays here? Sort of?

May as well make myself useful. There's lots to be done around here. Lots of little fix-up jobs I can attend to for my Dad. See you later.

See you.

Lucie takes her coffee and wanders into the living room. Sits down on the chesterfield. Can hear her father malign it in his large, scornful voice. Her father, who has no use for anything that hasn't had a big price tag attached. Her mother would say, Now Mel, just because people don't live as you do. He'd laugh loudly and say, That's for sure. You speak the truth, my love. Once in a while you get it right. Then her mother would blush—in pleasure or in anger? It was hard to tell—and not speak for an hour. In the end, he'd call her stupid about something and they'd be back where they started. Cat and mouse.

"Brr Nellie." "Old man." What's with you, Mitchell? she wonders. Whose voice am I hearing? Who knows? she answers herself, sighing. But maybe, just maybe, he is looking a little happier. That is surely something.

On the pale green walls of the living room are five pictures of dogs with dead things in their mouths. A fox. Ducks. A huge pink salmon. The centre painting is of a dog tugging the body of a child from a lake. The child is not actually dead, but close, from the colour of her and the way her eyes are rolled back. The dog, a gigantic black labrador, is on shore, and the child's sodden skirt is like papier-mâché against her legs. These are pictures of dogs that were pets when Mitchell was growing up, he has told her. Blackie. Mitzi. Brownie. Boots. Each painting has a wooden plaque below, with the dog's name on it in scrolled black ink, and thick coats of varnish on top of that. Dogs that for posterity had been invested with honour and valour befitting their spirits, if not their actions. Hunting, fishing, and life-saving skills copied from magazines onto the canvas by the loving hand holding the pastel. Mitchell's father's hand. Then frames, by Woolco.

Who would paint Spot the dalmatian's picture when the time came? Mitchell?

A stereo consul below the pictures, and those awful white and lime green nylon doilies that match the walls. The chesterfield and chairs, upholstered in green and gold flowers, are aimed at the rabbit-eared television.

How are you doing, dear?
It's freezing here, Mum. I miss you.
We miss you too dear. How are things going? Do you like the place?
Well, Dad would say it's all gingham and polyester and Safeway paintings. But really, it's okay. It has a certain charm. It's just different. Mitchell loves it. He loves everything about it.
Well, it's his home.
Mum, Mitchell still thinks his parents are going to show up. But how do you misread "missing and presumed dead"?
If he wants to badly enough, he can.
Christmas is going to be horrible.
Have you received our little package yet?
No. Nothing's come except snow.
Well, you wait for our little package, and maybe that'll help some. And go into Calgary, Lucie. Do a bit of shopping. I'm sure there's a Holt Renfrew there. And for shoes, try a place called Churgin's. Mary Beth used to live in Calgary— she's full of ideas. I'll tell you more next time we talk.
Mum, I wonder sometimes if Mitchell even knows I'm here. He wanders around outside all the time. And it's freezing out there.
It'll get better. He's having a bad time. You're a brave girl. Not too long now and you'll be home. We'll call you on Christmas, if we can get through.

Mitch? Are there Christmas decorations from when you were a boy that you'd like me to put up for you?
Mitch looks hesitant, doubtful. I wouldn't know where to find them.
I could help look. There's a bunch of stuff in the basement. And the attic.

What were you doing up there?
Just looking around.
Well, I wish you wouldn't. It doesn't seem right.
Mitchell, nothing seems right.
What do you mean?
It feels as though there's this shadow of wrongness creeping slowly over everything. Like a glacier. Do you feel it? It's giving me the creeps.
I don't feel anything.
Never mind. I just wanted to make things a little more like Christmas; I don't feel like it's Christmas at all. But if it troubles you, I'll stay out of the attic. What do you think we should do for decorations?
We'll wait. If they come home, they'll help us.
Mitch—
Don't say it.

The box that comes with UPS is enormous. Expertly packed by her mother, it is chock full of presents and Christmas trimmings, right down to shortbreads and a rum-soaked Christmas pudding from London Importers.

Look, Mitch! See what Mum's sent! There's everything here. Crackers. Cake. Pudding. She's so good, isn't she? Mum. She can tell without asking what we need, can't she? Look at these garlands! I know where she got these. She's been at the gift shop at the Vancouver Museum. She goes there every year and she knows I love their stuff. And look at this holly, Mitch! And smell this cedar! I guess we'll have to do without a tree, but that's okay. We'll live. Hey. Where are you going?

Lucie arranges cedar boughs on the mantelpiece, holly above the paintings in the living room, mistletoe in the archway into the dining room. Puts potpourri on the stove, and the house fills with aromas of cinnamon and orange, cranberry, fir, and cedar. She lines up all the baking on the kitchen counters.

On the linoleum floor at her feet, Spot thumps his tail.

It's going to be Christmas, she says to him. Do you know what that means, Spot? Smell it. See it. Warm hearts and happy times. Okay, good dog? Family. New times. You. Me. Mitchell.

Late that evening, she can't sleep. She never can, if Mitchell's not there with her. She goes out to the top of the stairs and sits. She sees him. Sees him morosely taking bits of holly down. She watches as he jams them painfully into the front pockets of his jeans. Why doesn't he just throw them away? she wonders. Why the need for more pain?

And she quietly rises and goes back to bed. And cries, because she doesn't know how to help him. Because she knows she's tried too hard, gone overboard with the decorations and doesn't know how to back up. Because he hurts so much and she can't find a way to help him.

I'm sorry I'm no fun, says Mitchell at breakfast. I can see how hard you're trying. I'm having a tough time getting used to all this. Being here. You know.

Then he shows her a line of trees out the kitchen window. Know what those are? he asks.

No. Spruce? I can't tell from here.

Those are Christmas trees. My dad plants them. Every spring he plants a seedling at that end, and every Christmas, he cuts one from this end. That second one there is this year's. I'll go get it for you after breakfast, if you want. Guess I'll just leave the other standing.

Excellent. I'll come with you. I can hold the tree steady while you cut it down.

Um, I think I'd rather do it alone, if you don't mind. It's something—my dad and I used to do it, you see.

Sure. I just thought—

Spot will help me though, won't you, boy? And then I've got to go into town. Do some shopping.

She serves Christmas dinner in the small white dining room Mitchell's father built his wife eleven years ago for their thirtieth anniversary. They eat on the Memory Lane china Lucie takes from the built-in china cabinet, on the table laid on their wedding white linen cloth with its padded silencer underneath, and with the wild rose silver plate flatware from its cherry wood box. They drink wine from a set of four sherry glasses Mitchell, oddly, has given her for Christmas—she has never been a sherry drinker. She has a *Farmer's Almanac* too, and, again oddly, a compass.

Mitchell, never a big talker, forks in his dinner with morose gusto, all the while attempting to articulate his hope and his grief. He gets very drunk on red wine, spills it down the front of the Pendleton wool shirt she has given him.

Luce, you don't understand—

I'm trying, Mitch.

Can't. No way. Luce, you just can't understand. I never should have bought the tickets. What a stupid idea.

It wasn't stupid, Mitchell. It was a good idea.

Oh right, he says with a snark. Just brilliant. Nope. You just can't understand. Can you? He fills his glass.

Another glass or two later, Mitchell gets down on his hands and knees to retrieve his serviette, and falls asleep under the table.

Lucie leaves him, sits on the wooden stool in the kitchen and looks out the window, at the flat grey light on the cold and snowy ground. At home in Vancouver, her parents and her brother will be playing Scrabble and drinking hot spicy wine. Her mother objecting quietly to someone's—probably her father's—use of American spelling, and her father perusing the dictionary with his annual Christmas cigar champed between his teeth. A huge fire in the stone fireplace, and the two Brittany spaniels chewing new squeaky toys.

No call comes. Lucie tries to call them, but can't get through. Her brother Les will miss her. She misses him. She stares over at the tree. Les has sent a small table lamp, made from driftwood. She's always been the buffer between him and her father. What will happen this year? Dear Les. Quiet, gay, gentle Les. He bends utterly under their father's rough words. Jellyfish, her father calls it with contempt. Pliant, she calls it.

Les had begun to be saved when he landed a job as a wharfinger on Galiano Island. He lives on his boat now; lives alone, travelling to Salt Spring once a week for a shower. Since putting the distance between himself and their father, he has relaxed, seems happier. She wants very much to see him, hug him hard and long. Oh Les. It's been almost a year.

But here she is in Dahlia, with Mitchell passed out beside his big fat dog, the two of them snoring. Red wine is spilled on Mitchell Mama's white linen cloth. Lucie reads the outside thermometer—thirty below, Fahrenheit. The trees near the house have white velvet antlers. Ice fog blocks the road and the sky. The yard lights go out and the hall light comes on in the same instant. She buttons up her mother's present, a purple angora cardigan. Puts her cheek against its softness. Leafs through the *Gourmet* cookbook also sent by her mother. Lingers over the pictures of truffles, longs for salmon mousse, and Grand Marnier soufflé; here is a plenitude of recipes for rich and luscious food, food that makes her mouth water and her senses swell. She uses her father's Christmas cheque as a bookmark.

JANUARY

Cooking becomes easier as she grows accustomed to the kitchen's layout, even with the unfamiliar utensils and the curious rhythms required to move from one cupboard to the next. At their place in Vancouver, she engaged in dance when she cooked—cupboards and drawers arranged so she moved easily from counter, to refrigerator, to stove. Pots came to one hand, whisks and spoons to another in wide smooth motions. Here, she reached, put down, climbed on a stool, reached, put down, in graceless combinations.

But both the wood and the gas stoves are excellent, and Lucie's completely overcome her fear of using them. The knives are sharp, and varied. Overall, from what she can tell, it's a well-stocked kitchen, though some things are showing signs of age. At lunchtime one day as she sets the table she says, These dishes are nice, but they're getting pretty ancient, Mitch, aren't they? Let's go into the city this afternoon and pick out some new ones. We need to go in for groceries anyway.

There's nothing wrong with these.

Almost all of them are chipped at least a little, and plenty of them are cracked.

I've got a lot to do this afternoon, Lucie.

Mitch—if they come back, they have new dishes—what's so bad about that?

You know, says Mitchell, I can remember the day these dishes were delivered by the Sears truck. I can still see Mum's face. She was so pleased. Thought Dad had spoiled her rotten.

Mitch? Lucie asks, coming over to the table, resting her hands on Mitchell's shoulders. She knew that's all he had wanted. To spoil them just a little. Send them on a holiday. Mitch, I was just wondering. Have you been keeping in touch with the Hawaii police?

Yes. They have my number. And address.

Nothing yet, then?

Nothing yet.

I wonder how long we should wait.

Lucie ladles mushroom soup into bowls. Puts a plate of devilled eggs on the table, a bowl of potato salad made with his mother's recipe, sandwiches made with Black Forest ham on fresh rye bread.

It must have been hard to be a farmer's wife, she says, taking off her apron and sitting down.

Why?

Getting useful things for presents all the time. Stuff you need, never stuff you want just for wanting's sake. Dishes. Mixmasters. I'd hate that.

Mitchell's face looks suddenly like thunder. He says, Things can be functional and attractive at the same time, you know.

I'm sorry. You're right. Maybe I'm spoiled. Boy, this soup is excellent; your Mum was quite the cook, wasn't she?

She sure . . . was. The word is barely audible.

Lucie decides to try again.

You know, Mitch, I can picture her—your Mama—here in the kitchen sometimes. Sometimes I even talk to her. I can picture her working away over these stoves, in these ovens. It would be such hard work. And then the men would come in to eat, without even getting cleaned up first. They'd work, eat, then back out to work again. Barely a visit. Then she'd be left alone again. There would be no romance whatsoever in such an existence, would there? She'd have to create her own, if she wanted any.

It wasn't anything like that. You have to grow up in a farming family to understand.

Maybe. But I still feel this sadness, somehow.

He stands up suddenly, fast. Shoves his chair away from the table. The chair leg catches the table leg; the table careens and the salt and pepper and one of the coffee cups and saucers crash to the floor.

Look, Lucie. She was *happy*.

He kicks the pepper mill under the stove.

I'm sorry. All I meant was not everyone would be happy in this life. That's all I meant. Really. I'm sorry.

This isn't *Madame Bovary*, Lucie. Not everyone wants romance up the ying yang. Not *everyone* is appalled at the thought of actually helping their mate. Pitching in together for a common goal. That's what farm life is about.

Mitch—

My mother *likes* to cook, she *likes* to gather the eggs, she *likes* living here! And she likes to help my Dad, in case you haven't noticed. You. Whining for your lace tablecloths and your cappuccino machine. My mother will sure have something to say about *that*, I'll tell you.

Now Mitchell kicks the saltcellar across the room, grabs his coat from the hook and goes out, yanking the door behind him, leaving Lucie startled, hurt, surprised. He talked about his parents in the present tense. As though they weren't missing. Weren't dead.

Lucie stands outside, feels the cold permeate her flesh. She can see her breath; God it can be cold here. She rubs her hands together. Wishes she had remembered her mitts.

Mitchell? she says to the closed, apparently barricaded barn door, and her words come out in fog. Mitch, are you there?

There is no sound from the other side.

The sky is low and grey; almost touches the top of her head. Spot nudges her with his nose; licks her freezing hands.

Back in the house, she feels desire rise like bread dough. She pushes it down, down, but still it rises. She does want her things in Vancouver. Her Cuisinart. Her espresso machine. Her grandmother's afghan. Even her vacuum cleaner. Because it's hers, because she knows the feel of its handle, the motor's sound.

She aches to say to Mitchell, Take me *home*. Wants to whine, When are we going *home*, as she did as a child. Longs to tell him that for her, death has touched each bite they eat, that the ghosts of his missing parents watch and judge her from every cracked and chipped plate, every cupboard, every window. And the longer they stay here, the worse things become. This isn't healing; he isn't getting better.

As one day follows another, she learns it is *not* okay to empty a drawer in the bathroom to make more room for their toiletries, or to move his father's cardigan from the back of the kitchen chair, or the winter boots from the back door. It is not okay to rearrange cupboards, though washing and ironing the kitchen curtains is fine, dusting is fine, vacuuming is fine. Mitch hasn't noticed she is wearing his mother's aprons. Or maybe that is fine too.

If in doubt, ask, Mitchell said, hands shaking as he replaced the sweater and smoothed its shoulders.

Mitch? How long do you think we should stay?

Do we have to talk about that right now?

I'm sorry. But I have to tell my clients something. It's been a month.

He stands abruptly and clears the table. Cereal bowls, spoons, plates clatter in the sink. Hot water rushes down on them, suds rise up in mounds. Silence.

Just leave them. I'll do the dishes, Mitch.

I always do the dishes. He grabs the dishcloth.

No you don't. We take turns.

Here, I do the dishes.

Oh. Okay.

She stands in the doorway with her coffee, watches him put his heart into this work.

She finishes up her last two projects on her pocketbook computer, goes into the city and sends them off. She reads the piles of *Reader's Digest*. She looks through all the cookbooks, all the gardening books. She cleans house and makes Mitchell meals. She doesn't follow her mother's urging, doesn't go into town to find some "decent" shops. What for? They don't go anywhere, except out in the yard. What use finery on a farm? No point at all. Instead she enters recipes asterisked by Mitchell's mother onto her computer.

Mitchell fixes all the drips in all the taps. Then he moves on to squeaks, the outside steps, and the inside stairs.

She is sure she hears him say under his breath, You've been wanting this done for some time now, haven't you? as he oils the hinges on the screen door.
What did you say, Mitchell?
Nothing.
Mitchell lies with his back against hers, as cool as the white cotton sheets. She moves her hand up under his pajama top, and her fingers follow the bumps in his spine from sternum to skull and down again, pausing at nape and the base of his spine to brush the soft hair. Then she curls up close to him, his buttocks fleshy and strong against her belly. Oh how she wants him. Longs for him. It's been too long. She slips her hands round the front of him, to his flat stomach, traces the ridge of hair there, from navel to groin. She feels his penis stir.
Don't, he says.
I want you, she says. Let's make up and fool around.
Don't, he says.
Don't. Don't. Say *do*, okay? Come on, love. I miss you.
Stop it, he says.
She pauses, pulls away, lies still.
After a couple of minutes he says, Lucie? I'm staying.
Staying? *Here*?
Yes.
What about work?
I called today and quit. I'll get UIC.
But what about my work?
You'll have to decide.
Turn over, Mitch. Look at me!
I'm staying, he says, still turned away. That's all I know.
Look at me!
Finally he rolls over.
For how long?
Lucie, I don't know.
Do you want me? Do you want me to stay?

Of course I want you to stay.
Then will you hold me, Mitch? Please?
I'm really beat, Luce.
We don't have to do anything. Just hold me. You're not alone.
All right.
Mitchell whistles as he brings up tool boxes and paint from the basement. He touches up the paint (yellow cream) in the bathroom, regrouts the tub (harvest gold) and the tile (daisies and grain), scrubs down the glass and aluminum sliding shower door (stained, ugly, constantly sticking).

There's plenty to keep me busy until it's time to get out in the fields, he says one day. Then adds, Boy, I never thought I'd hear myself say something like that.

Didn't you say the land is leased?

It is. To the Wreggits. Their son Lorne was my high school buddy, as a matter of fact. Slick mover that guy. Didn't think he'd still be around. Anyway, I can offer to give them a hand. Can always use another man. I'm going to go over and talk to them about it later on. Find out what they're planting this year. You know, I never thought I'd look forward to spring the way I am. Before, I would do anything to get off this farm.

Well, good. I called my mother. She'll arrange to have our clothes sent, to start with. By next week.

That'll make you happy.

Mitch? Don't you miss our place? The ocean? The English Bay Cafe?

Can't hardly picture them anymore.

I'm trying to get used to seeing this as our new home. It'll take some getting used to. For me. I've never lived anywhere like this—we're so far away from everything. And Mitch? I know it'll be hard for you, but we will really *have* to sit down and figure out how we're going to accommodate all this *stuff*.

What stuff?

Our stuff. Their stuff.
What's for lunch?
Quiche. I've never made one before. This one is leek and mushroom. I got the recipe from that cookbook Mum sent me for Christmas.
That fancy one?
You're a little like a leek, you know. Long and white. And mild. Though you used to be milder, I think.
You're pretty funny, Luce.
And hard when you're raw. I like you both ways, you know. Ha ha.

She holds the receiver away from her ear.
After we educated you at that fancy goddamn design school you're dumping it all to live on a goddamn *farm*? Pack your work in just when it gets rolling to gather eggs and shovel cow shit with that farmboy?
Dad, it's not like that.
I'm disappointed in you, Lucie. I'm sure as shit disappointed in you. And so is your mother.
Lucie dear? Her mother is on another phone, listening, waiting for a chance to speak. Lucie, he's upset. Your father's upset, dear. That's all. He'll be all right.
Mitch buries himself in his work, doesn't notice when she comes up behind him, pees right beside him and flushes the toilet. Little beads of sweat deck his brow. Next, he removes the glass door knobs from all the inside doors of the house, shines the brass plating, polishes the glass before replacing them. Glides around her like a distracted ghost.

FEBRUARY

A deep chinook arch reaches wide across the sky. The temperature has soared to well above freezing. Water drips from the eaves, Spot basks his tubby body in the sun on the porch. Lucie finds herself humming "Oh My Darling Clementine."

Mitchell actually hops out of his truck; there is bounce in his step as he approaches the house. He stands straighter, something resembling happiness in his eyes.

Guess what? I was just over at the Wreggits. They want me to take their dogs. All of them. Ten. They say they're getting on. The dogs are too much work, and Lorne doesn't want them. Lucie. I can buy their whole darn kennel.

Wow. I thought you went over there to talk about *farming*.

I did. They're putting in a field of peas this year, along with the flax and the wheat. And the canola, of course.

Oh. That sounds good. I guess. Hey, I didn't know you liked dogs that much.

I've wanted to raise dogs since I was a kid.

What kind of dog?

Rottweilers. I'm nuts about them.

Rottweilers? Aren't they mean? And ugly?

Mitchell sighs deeply. I love the look of them, Lucie, he says plainly. And they aren't as mean as you think. They aren't mean at all, if you're kind to them. These are great dogs. Please don't give me a hard time. Please?

Okay, she thinks, biting her lip.

Okay, she says, and then he tells her about building the accommodations, exercise runs, by modifying the barn. Maybe he'll put in a grooming centre, later on.

Well, keep the noise down as much as you can, all right? she says, feeling like a parent. Face the exercise runs away from the house, to keep it as quiet as you can, would you?

Sure thing, honey, he says, and kisses her soundly on the cheek.

Cabbage. Lucie is quartering a tender young head of cabbage when, clean and shaven, in a clean white shirt and jeans, Mitchell comes into the kitchen.

Yikes. She feigns surprise. What happened to you?

Thought I'd better clean up my act a little. I'm sorry, Lucie, for the times I'm a jerk. Thanks for putting up with me. With one hand he touches her waist. With the other, he holds out a pot. A white lily.

For you. Happy Valentine's Day.

She's touched by this gesture. Made hopeful. Maybe the old Mitchell is coming back. Thank-you, Mitchell, she says. Thank-you very much.

You're welcome. I'd be happy to help with supper, too. If you want.

—

I would. Try me.

Okay. Get the cauliflower out of the fridge. Wash and trim it. I'm going to steam the cabbage, then saturate it with butter, lemon juice, and white pepper. Sound good?

Yessir. What else we having?

Tarragon noodles in cream sauce. You could cook the pasta when you're done with the cauliflower.

Sure.

I'll do the fish, and the sauce. It's just a mix, but it looks good from the picture.

Side by side, across from each other, around each other, they work. The kitchen windows are open; a curtain brushes against the the ceramic eggplant. She's thrown out the broken carrots, and only the cabbage and eggplant remain in the small wicker basket. The cabbage always looks grubby; it catches dirt in its ridges, and its colour is wrong, more like an avocado than a cabbage. One of these days she'll accidently drop it and that'll leave the eggplant alone. The eggplant she likes. Likes its cool roundness. Sometimes she takes it out of the nest and rubs its belly against her own.

Mitch cuts the cauliflower into tiny little pieces. The pasta cooks for half an hour. But she says nothing. Everything will be fine.

Wine?

Bottle of white in the fridge. French, I think. Good for the sole. Pan fried fillets of sole. I bought a new cookbook when I went into town to buy coffee. *The Sixty Minute Gourmet.* I'm beginning to like being out here, you know. The traffic really gets to me once I'm in the city now. And all the people around everywhere. Impossible to find a place to park.

The table is set, by Mitchell, while she dips the fish in egg, flour, milk, and crumbs, sautés it lightly in butter, sprinkles it with bits of lemon flesh and capers. The table's white cloth is laid with the new white dishes, about which Mitchell has said nothing. The white lily sits in the middle. She stands in the doorway with the bottle of sauterne. And starts to cry. Holds the bottle up against her hot cheeks to help her stop, but can't. Nothing she does seems to work. Something always goes wrong.

When do we eat? says Mitchell.

You have to be anaemic to come to dinner, she says softly.

Why's that? What's the matter?

The whole dinner's going to be white. Cauliflower, cabbage, sole, noodles, pickled onions, dishes, serviettes, wine. People. White.

Mitchell smiles warily. It smells wonderful, he says. I could put on a red shirt.

Never mind.

Luce? Will you—

Will I what?

Never mind. Let's eat. I'm starved. Looks fine, he says. Don't worry about it.

Hey, Rapunzel, Mitchell says, coming up behind her. He reaches around and takes her silver-backed brush from the dressing table. He pulls the pins from her hair and it falls down her back. God your hair is gorgeous, he says, lifting it to his face. As they watch themselves in the mirror of her dressing table, he brushes her hair.

Long smooth strokes from crown down her back. He brushes gently up and back from her jaw, then across each temple and back. Her head falls from one side to the other, forward and back. He smoothes, first with the palm of his hand, and then with the brush, from her forehead back, each hand taking a turn. Then rolling her hair up into a chignon, gently pulling her head back, he kisses her upside down. Dear one, he says. I've missed you. And he slips a hand inside the kimono's silk and onto her breast.

Dream on.
Mitchell did not come up behind her.
There is no dressing table, no silver-backed brush, no kimono. There is just Lucie, lying on the bed by herself, lying on her back while her heart pumps liquid disappointment, while she chastises herself for the dinner she made. After they ate, Mitchell said, Good supper. Then he did the dishes, took a beer into the living room, and studied his dog books. Fell asleep on the chesterfield. She lies on her back, runs the fingers of both hands gently over her face, traces her hairline, her eyebrows, her cheekbones, circles her mouth.

MARCH

The rag mats beside Mitchell Mama and Papa's bed and the brown and beige braided rug in the centre of the room are identical to the ones in the kitchen. The drapes and pictures have to be from the catalogue; where else? On the bureau a small bottle of White Shoulders, and a porcelain boy blowing a chipped horn. On the window sill a row of dusty, empty Avon bottles. Lucie sits on the bed, wondering about the absence of photographs in this house. There are no photographs in the bedroom. There are no photographs anywhere. This she finds both strange and frustrating—she still has no idea what his parents looked like. Oh Mitchell Mama, she says to the air. How was your life?

She pranced in here with nothing on but a towel, on her way to the bath. Came to an abrupt halt in front of his mother's mirror, startled in the discovery that she didn't look as she thought she did. She dropped the towel to peruse herself closely. How long is her back, how broad her rib cage. She imagined herself as lush, narrow, and lean—and getting leaner—from the front and the side, like a piece of river grass. How long had it been since she saw herself? She is more fleshy than she had pictured, more succulent than vine. Ballerina in a jewel box, she stood on her tiptoes and turned. She is not wasting away, after all. Pink and white person, pink and white woman. Pushing, pushing thirty.

In her own family, there are drawers full of pictures intended for walls, a desk top, a free counter space once an appropriate frame is found and purchased. Her father's study and her mother's sewing room are coated with pictures of her and her brother Les, of the family all together on this holiday or that. One or more of the four of them peering out from almost every wall of the house, bathroom included.

Her brother Les, with their mother's meek eyes, their father's sturdy build, always standing beside their mother, while her place is next to their father. Or in between. She has her mother's finer bones. Her father's determined eyes. And, lately, her very own trace of sadness.

Poor Les. Used to exude sadness. Hounded by their father for as long as she can remember. For not being this, failing to be that. *I'm goddamn well disappointed in you, Lucie.* Makes her glad there's some distance. Les sees almost no one through the winter months on the island. Just their parents, at Christmas. He's found happiness through solitude. She's beginning to understand.

Mitchell's father's drawers are full of stacks of polka dot handkerchiefs and white Stanfield undershirts and shorts. Suspenders. Boring. Tucked under his underwear a receipt for a fifty pound bag of flour, and a circle of safety pins, carefully graded, strung through the gills like fish on a length of cord. And dozens of socks, mostly grey work socks with a red stripe around the top, rolled into pairs. One pair of navy nylon dress socks. One pair of black.

In his mother's underwear drawer old lady panties and brassieres. Two pair of Supphose rolled up and two pair still in their packaging, Christmas gift cards taped on. Love, Lillian: Have a Merry Christmas. Two stale lavender sachets.

The rest of his mother's drawers contain considerably less intrigue. The meagerness of the woman's wardrobe is perhaps the most striking feature. How a woman lived her life with just four pairs of socks, for example, and two pairs of stockings. One half slip, five scarves—four pastel, and one black. Of course she'd have some things with her, but still. Two sweaters, and mothballs, in the bottom drawer.

At the front of the closet, below five cotton house dresses and three blouses—one short-sleeved, two long—are three pairs of shoes. Oomphies. Her husband has more clothes than she. Had, rather, Lucie reminds herself. His side is almost full, with one navy suit, and maybe a dozen flannel work shirts. The kind Mitchell has taken to wearing.

Not one picture. Anywhere. She wonders if they took pictures of each other in Hawaii. If their camera, if they even had one, would ever be found. When will the contents of their hotel room be forwarded—the clothes they weren't wearing? What's happened to them? Nothing has ever come. That she knows of. Maybe Mitch has never asked. She lies back on their bed, covers herself with the towel.

Mitchell's parents were lifted up into the sky and transported at jet speed to the lush heart of an extravagant luau. And then they vanished. Right off the beach. Giant flying palm trees swept down, wrapped them in their long frondy clutches, and off they sailed, deeper and deeper into the blue and romantic sky, further and fur-

ther into their concept of Paradise. One of his mother's sandals fell off at several thousand feet. Fell. Fell, like a lump of sea gull poop, until, finally, it smacked into the sea, and floated, being cork and plastic, for months on end. The name and address tag (one was carefully glued on each of her possessions) remained adhered in spite of the salt. Perhaps some day Lucie and Mitchell will receive a postcard in the mail from someone in Indonesia who had found the shoe washed up, and the postcard will be a complaint about cluttering foreign shores.

Cold, Lucie gets up from the bed and takes Mitchell Mama's plaid flannel dressing gown off the hook on the back of the door. Hope you don't mind, Mitchell Mama, she says to the air. I'm freezing. She pulls the sash tight around her waist and turns around in front of the mirror. She takes some of the hairpins from the china box in front of her, holds a few of the pins in her mouth while she tries to put her hair up in a bun. Not as easy as it looks, Mama, she says to herself in the mirror. Is it?

A few minutes later, she stands again in the closet, wondering what on earth they should do with these things. Then she hears Mitchell's voice.

Is there something I can help you with? His voice comes coldly, like some snobby salesman's, and, flushing hot with guilt, she backs out of the closet. He stands in the doorway of the bedroom, filling it with his body, sealing it shut. She feels a wave of menace, then of sorrow.

Is there something I can help you with, Lucie? he says again.

Yes, is what she would like to say. Yes, you could help me move these people out of here. They left all this stuff behind and there's nowhere for me, you see. For us. Let me explain. Have you got a minute? My lover and I are trying to nest, and it's becoming increasingly difficult to do. Mitchell-birds seem to have trouble mating in ancestral homes. Have you any advice?

I was wondering why there aren't any photographs, actually, she says uncomfortably.

He shifts slightly, crosses his arms. She can see slivers of light at his waist. You could have just asked me, he says, looking right at her. She casts her eyes down, feels like a bad child about to get a lecture, then a slap.

How would you like someone going through your stuff? His eyes slowly examine her hair, the dressing gown, and how it is opened almost fully to her breastbone, revealing much of her breasts. He looks abruptly away.

As a matter of fact, Lucie, they thought pictures vain. They weren't religious nuts or anything, if that's what you're thinking. Somewhere we'll probably come across a few, I'll bet. Without snooping. My parents—modest people, he says, struggling. There's a wedding picture somewhere. I've seen it. And a few of me. My school pictures. And one or two birthdays. He pauses. Looks piercingly at her again. Take off my mother's dressing gown, he says. Now.

He remains in the doorway until she steps out of the room, wrapped once again in a towel. Shivering. He closes the door firmly behind him.

Good morning, Mitchell Mama, Lucie says to the air as she ties on Mitchell Mama's apron. I hope you don't mind if I call you that. It's very easy to believe you are still here, you know. I'm beginning to see how Mitchell does. He's acting odd though lately, don't you think? Have you noticed? I'm trying to hang in there, however. Tough it out, as my father would say. For lunch? I'm expanding my horizons. I'm going to try a special tropical spinach salad. Maybe you've had one like it—in Hawaii. And grilled cheese sandwiches with pimento and slivers of red onion. See the picture?

She feels a presence, turns around.

We call it dinner out here, says Mitchell. Supper's at night.

Mango, Orange, and Spinach Salad

8 oz fresh spinach—tear into bite-sized pieces
2 oranges—peel and section
2 mangoes—peel, cut flesh from pits, cut flesh into small chunks
$1/2$ cup thinly sliced mild onion
Dressing:
$1/2$ cup oil
$1/4$ cup fresh lime juice
$1/2$ tsp salt
$1/4$ tsp white pepper
$1/2$ tsp dry mustard

Method:
Combine dressing ingredients in a jar and shake. Pour dressing over salad ingredients to moisten as desired. Toss gently to mix well.

Sweaters, blouses, t-shirts. Wool pants, stirrup pants, summer dresses and shorts, and shoes, shoes, shoes. City clothes. She had forgotten she had most of them.

How should we do this, Mitchell? Where should we start?

Mitchell stares at his own clothes—his suits, his dress shirts and ties, his loafers, his trenchcoat—as though he doesn't know what they are.

Our *clothes*. We have to make room for our clothes, at least. All the closets are full. Mitch? Say something!

I'm thinking, he says evenly. Let me think, would you?

Okay, he says finally. Maybe we could move some stuff up to the attic. There's a big long bar up there to hang clothes on. I used to play circus up there.

Maybe you better show me what you want to move first. Good idea. Ask me. Yes.

She carries his high school hockey gear up the narrow

stairs, helmet on her head, shin pads under her arms. She carries an armload of boy's summer shirts and a Scout uniform. So his mother never got rid of anything either, she thinks. That's where he gets this; that's why he can't let go.

These clothes of his own he has given his approval to move. But when she comes out of his parents' room with his mother's dresses over her arm, he pales so much she thinks he's going to pass right out and fall down the stairs. What would he be like if clothes were to appear instead of disappear? she wonders.

Mitch? Did anything ever come from Hawaii? Any of their clothes? Anything at all?

No. Not yet.

Don't you think that's strange?

No, I don't.

APRIL

Under the cellar stairs, amid peat pots, potting soil, and gardening tools, Lucie finds a dozen bulbs. Probably bought by Mitchell Mama who knows when and forgotten, she decides. As the bulbs looked for what they need—for warmth, for light—they have sent out pale shoots into the cool and unreceptive darkness. Lucie decides to plant the bulbs anyway, and see what happens. She sets them carefully in the terra cotta pots she also finds; nourishes them with earth and moisture.

Tenderly she lifts the basket containing the ceramic eggplant from the window sill. If you were real, she says to it, you would need the sunshine. She sets the basket on the counter by her cookbooks. From time to time from now on she will pick up the eggplant and hold it in her hands, linger over the pleasing feel of its glossy belly. Dust it against her apron before placing it back in its basket.

She sets the pots on the kitchen window sill. Lo and behold the bulbs grow, surprisingly rapidly, surprisingly well.

Next, she will grow a garden. Her vegetables will be fresher, her salads more interesting with exotic lettuces and fresh herbs. She'll drive to Sunnsyide Nursery and get a catalogue, pore over that; grow whatever inspires her, whatever she desires. Maybe she'll try to grow eggplants, although she has never cooked with them. Her father has sent another cheque; his way of apologizing for his anger, his way of sending her love. That makes three. None cashed yet, and each enough to hold them for a month or more even without their UIC money. She'll cash them tomorrow. It's time to spend. Freely.

Outside, with shirts off and sawdust clinging to their sweat in an early false summer, Mitchell and his friend Lorne are building the forms for pouring the floors of the exercise runs; they have built kennel doors through the barn wall; they run out rolls of chain link. Lucie clears the vegetable garden of what detritus is left from last year's plants, pauses frequently to watch the men, too often catching Lorne watching her.

Who ever said labourers have no brains? Her father, probably. With pleasure Luce watches the two men solve problems with mind, with body. Clothe the naked idea, one of her teachers at design school used to say. She loves to watch Mitchell's lean brown movements.

On a particularly hot day, when the men are out of sight inside the barn, she lies in the warmed earth, face to the sun. Revels in the smell of freshly turned earth, and peat moss. Hears only the murmur of the men's voices, feels the warm breeze against her skin.

She and Mitchell are on a drive, and it is hot in the car. The only relief is when they temporarily enter the shadow of a mountain, once, twice, thrice. As the heat intensifies, Lucie suddenly wants him inside her like nothing on earth. She gazes out her window, indulging the feeling as he drives, his long capable fingers wrapped round the steering wheel. Foothills and mountains become breasts and groins; she sees cocks and balls in the clouds. She wants him to stop the car so they can couple. Wait, he says. Just wait, okay? Her skin presses against, melts into, the clear plastic seat covers, and she becomes hotter, and hotter. She tries to will one of his hands off the steering wheel and onto her crotch, but he doesn't move an inch. Images of succulence fill her mind; she sees warm, ripe cantaloupe breasts; she tastes juicy, hot, blackberry pie. Bake; boil into syrup; bubble over.

Deep in the forest Mitchell parks in the shade but inside the car it is still hot as an oven. She doesn't want to get out, wants to cook and respond like that pie, but the heat is unbearable. Mitchell is already out, standing in a breeze. She joins him and they stand side by side, arms around each other, at the shore of the small, still lake. Around her, flesh now appears in flowers, and branches, and in the shapes of leaves. Mitchell's body casts a long dark shadow onto the water. An eerie, intense bleating comes from the forest.

What's that noise? she whispers.

Elk, he says. Elk, rutting.

She reaches for him and says, I want to rut. Right here. On this moss.

He smiles. Oh yeah?

She can almost feel his cock entering, pushing into her, hot, and moist, and hard.

Fuck me, Mitchell; fuck me hard, she whispers. Make me a furry calf; make me a wet black cub.

His smile fades. Wait, Lucie, he says. Wait.

When she opens her eyes, the men are coming out of the barn with shovels. Through one open eye she watches their loins as they walk towards her.

Turn your garden for you, ma'am? says Lorne with a grin, winking both eyes.

Once the dogs arrive—on a noisy Tuesday afternoon—Mitchell spends even more time away from the house, feeding, watering, stroking. Crooning to all ten of them. She's heard him through the barn door when she goes out to call him in for meals.

Broiled Tomato Soup

½ cup butter
2 T olive oil
1 large onion, sliced
1 tsp fresh dill
1 tsp fresh thyme
1 tsp fresh basil
¼ tsp. white pepper
8 medium Roma tomatoes
3 T tomato paste
¾ c chicken stock
1 cup whipping cream
½ cup fresh parmesan cheese

The broiler is hot. Lucie has pureed the Italian tomato soup, grated the parmesan, whipped the cream. All that is left to do is to blend the whipped cream and parmesan, glob it onto the soup ladled into bowls, and run them under the broiler. Dill bread is on the table, wrapped in a linen cloth to keep it warm. The caesar salad needs shaking in its bag, and then *voilà*.

She stops briefly to stand at the screen door and listen to Mitchell. He's on the porch, down on the painted wooden floor, leaned up against the exterior wall of the house. Spot is turned up between his legs, and he is brushing the dog's belly. The other dogs, jealous and mournful, stand at the chain link fence in the yard by the barn, wagging their nubby tails hopefully. Spot is relaxed to his toes. Upside down, his lips and cheeks fall away from big white teeth, pink tongue peeks out between them. His eyes are rolled halfway back. Such a grin makes him look mad.

You're a sweetie, aren't you? What a good dog you are, Mitchell says. She watches his hands stroke, stroke the fur. The dog wriggles with pleasure, licks his fingers. Mitchell fingers the ear so gently, strokes the black nose.

Inside, Lucie's hands loosely roam her rounding belly. How well she's eating these days. She crosses her hands and runs them up her sides, over her breasts. How ripe and warm she is. And the inside of her upper arms, and the inside of her thighs—open, open—her skin is so smooth. Her bones are awake, her deep purple, musty-scented skin is ready to burst, spill its hundreds of seeds, send them flying.

The first time another's hands touched her entire flesh, her body and its sensations were as new to her as they were to him. She had never (don't touch yourself there) touched where he explored. How it all connected. What thigh against thigh, what chest against chest, can feel like, compared with a mouth on neck, on mouth, on breast; a hand between legs, in hair, along a side, or across a flat belly. Skin is different, somehow, when two naked bodies align. She and the boy lay in surprising stillness in which, ears ringing, almost too loud to bear, she could listen to her flesh, hear its being touched. It seemed that neither of them breathed. And then that welcome end of virginity.

She stretches her body and it curves upward. Enter my body. Someone. Anyone. Welcome trespass.

The wonderful smells she has created waft out into the porch and the yard. The dogs have all noticed—they are drooling heavily, with their noses raised—but Mitchell hasn't.

She returns to her cooking, folds the parmesan into the whipping cream. Blend. Whip. Pour. Stir.

Mitch? Supper's on the table.

Be right there.

It'll get cold.

Feed the animals first. My Dad taught me that.

Maybe he kisses them all goodnight, too. On the bridge of the nose. On that smooth place below the eye. At the corner of the mouth. Maybe they all kiss him back. Maybe that's why. . . .

She taps her wooden spoon on the edge of the bowl. Please Mitchell please please please won't you stroke my belly. Won't you please please please kiss me under my chin, kiss my ear, the nape of my neck.

She throws the spoon in the sink.

As April turns into May, Mitchell Mama's bulbs stop growing. The strong green leaves of the tulips unfurl and grow tall, stalks sturdy and green. A hyacinth grows cupped like a crocus until it reveals the tip of its flower head. Then they all pause. The flower heads try to open, but can't. The red and yellow stripe of one tulip, the eggplant purple of the other, are tinged with brown like an onion's skin. Green stamen poke through the shrivelled and malformed petals. Look naked. Vulgar. The hyacinth remains a tiny cob of purple corn hidden deep in a circle of six green leaves.

MAY

Lucie opens the kitchen window wide to bring in a breeze and leans out; the air is heavy and warm. Early summer and hope. The eggplants and green peppers have sprouted in their peat pots. She will transplant them into the garden soon. She has already planted rows of lettuce, of carrots, potatoes, and peas in the well-turned earth, and marked each row. This weekend she'll do the herbs. Inside, in milk cartons with a Tums in the bottom of each, her tomato plants are doing well, sitting in the sun on the window sills. The earth in the milk cartons is warm, and she can smell it, smell the peat with the slightly bitter tomato plant smell.

Above her garden, beyond the buildings, the world is so very flat. Clear through. You wouldn't notice it so much if you live in the city, wouldn't realize the bigness of the uninterrupted sky, wouldn't see the huge storm fronts moving in and moving away. The uncomplicated, uninterrupted vastness exhilarates.

She sees herself out in the yard. A younger self; she is clapping her mitts together. She's wearing her grey duffel coat, the one with the bone catches, the one left over from her boarding school uniform. She taps hard on the window, waves at herself. Herself looks too far up and doesn't see her. She smiles, taps again. Look up! From Sunday school on, up the direction you look to seek and find Good. The direction of Grownups and Hope. Head up. Chin up. Look up; look waaaay up. She waves at herself again. Herself lowers her gaze, sees her, waves back. She has lifted the hood of her coat and latched the strap across her chin. The wind has picked up, is biting her cheeks.

Herself starts walking towards the kennel. Now, sensing a presence in the yard, the dogs start up barking like mad fools and herself turns back towards the house, rolling her eyes and grinning. Dogs. Herself hangs out her tongue in mock panting, tilts her head back in mock howl. Is lifted from the earth voice first, pulled through the sky as though she is born of Chagall, and disappears into the swirling white wisps of fine snow.

I don't want to go away to school, Dad.

But I want you to, Lucie-girl. You're not going to turn out like Les, and that's for damn sure. Hang in there. Tough it out and you'll learn to stick with things. You've got your old man's genes. Go on now. We'll see you at Easter. Chin up.

Inside the house, behind her, things are different. Chaotic. The counters are covered. With peels, flour, rolling pins, pastry cloth, cheese grater, garlic press, coffee mugs, silver polish, chamois, and flower stems. It has been one hell of a busy day. She is determined. She is going to knock Mitchell's socks off. And the rest of his clothes.

This morning Lucie made the dessert, which will *have* to blow him away:

Bombe Glacé

1 quart mocha ice cream, softened
¾ cup chopped almonds
1 quart chocolate ice cream, softened
1 pint honey vanilla ice cream, softened
2 tablespoons Tia Maria
2 ounces unsweetened chocolate, melted and cooled
¼ cup light corn syrup
1 egg

Method:
Soften, melt, blend; smooth, harden, fill; combine; spread. Garnish.

In the sieve in the sink the spinach drains. In the well-stoked wood stove, the salmon bakes. The soufflé dish is buttered and coated with fine bread crumbs. The gas oven and warming oven are heated and ready. The thickened cheese sauce waits on the stove. The egg whites are stiff in their bowl. The sound of the beaters has been all around, and now, instead of their racket, she hears Chopin.

White wine in the fridge, and the pickles in small Yugoslavian dishes. Pickled onions and baby carrots from the rows and rows of preserves and conserves downstairs.

In a plain sterling vase, two mauve freesia, their sweet, drugging scent. Lucie jubilant, high, trembling with pleasure at the food, the ambience, the place. The pale pink batik tablecloth looks lovely in the dining room; reflected light catches the cut glass and splatters light all over the walls.

Cups and saucers, gleaming coffee spoons, sugar and true cream on the sideboard. Dinner plates warming in the oven.

These are her dishes, her linen and silver. Her simple, elegant china, her Royal Doulton Sarabande, with its plain silver edges and bone whiteness. This table, these things, sent by her mother, or bought by Lucie in town, and the food she is preparing, please her beyond measure, beyond words. On the CBC the Chopin has ended, and Jurgen Gothe talks of sauterne for breakfast and the escapades of his cats. Then he plays a mazurka.

I am in my element, Lucie says to Mitchell Mama. I've found it. I love being here, you know. Pardon? Who is coming for dinner? Lovers, to be quite frank. *Unmarried* lovers, Mitchell Mama, who will start anew and see where that takes them.

As the sun sets, a grubby, distracted Mitchell in a flannel shirt and dirty jeans appears in the kitchen doorway. Two or three days' growth of beard on his face. He looks as though he's become his own shadow. He smells of dog so strongly the odour over-rides the freesia, the baking salmon, the garlic in the dressing.

Have you seen the cod liver oil? he asks.

No, she says.

I left it right there.

I haven't seen it.

I left it right there.

Aren't you going to get cleaned up for dinner?

When's dinner?

Soon.

I have to feed the animals first.

Lucie waits, fiddles with final preparations.

The soufflé falls.

The salmon dries.

You're part of this world, Mitchell Mama. How long does it take to feed ten dogs?
The bombe bombs.
Mitchell Mama, your son . . .
Breathe, Lucie, breathe deep, deep, she tells herself.
. . . is a Jerk. A Big Big Jerk.
Breathe deep from inside; throat ache, chest heave. I want to scream I want to scream my head off. Why am I doing this? Why oh why am I doing this?

The dinnered table. Forks and spoons lie in puddles of ice cream. Lucie's wine glass is half full with the heel of the wine. Red kisses around its crystal rim.
At the centre of the table the freesia droop low. The silver vase is tarnished yellow, as though she didn't polish it that very afternoon. And the tablecloth looks grey, almost mildewed.
Things between you and me are starting to stink as bad as that mushroom barn, Mitchell. I'm going to start not caring one of these days, you know. I can feel it. If that happens, Mitchell, if neither one of us cares, what do you suppose will happen then?
She watches his hands. They are tense and fidgeting, as though they are trying to articulate. These hands. Dexterous on barbed wire and electrical wiring. On picture frame nails, bits of plaster, glass. With hammers, screwdrivers, drills. These hands. In their apartment, bending her over the divan, holding her hips while he thrust.
You always make everything black or white, he says. With you, everything's always all bad.
In this case it happens to be true. We're like those rows of pickled walnuts downstairs. Black. Smelly. Falling apart.
If you say so.
So I see. So I hear. Can't you tell? Mitch, how long has it been since you touched me?
Give me some space, Lucie.

Space! I hardly ever see you. Lay *my* carpet, Mitchell. Scratch *my* belly.

He doesn't answer. Scowls at his plate.

Baby, my sweet baby, You're the most, sings K.T. Oslin, and the ache between Lucie's legs is in K.T.'s voice. The ache between Lucie's legs is in Lucie's heart, in her head, in the food she prepares, in every movement of her body.

Always feed the animals first, she says to herself in the mirror. His father taught him that.

The mirror replies, Feed yourself.

JUNE

June. The garden coming up, the snow coming down like crazy, and starting to drift. Shoots newly pushed through the earth now waver in the snow, even as it falls against that tender, cold greenness. In her garden, one small fern she foolishly planted on a whim, weighted down with wet snow. Lettuce. Beans. Peas. The eggplant seedlings. All invisible now. Daffodils and tulips, up to their necks in snow blown against the house.

Spring. Such an enormous amount of pain involved with all that birthing. Forcing down and up and through. Ewes, and cows, and hyacinths. Forced. Through flesh, through earth, through harder things, if need be. Lucie, looking out a window in the bedroom as the spring storm turns green to white, blue to white. Shivers. Holds her hands against her belly. Buttons up her purple cardigan.

Sautéed Young Asparagus

16 tender stalks of young asparagus
1 ½ tsp Dijon mustard
1 small onion, minced

Method:
Melt two tablespoons of butter in a medium skillet and sauté onions. Add asparagus and sauté gently until tender. Stir in mustard and let stand for 2 to 3 minutes.

Spot sleeps in a gold overstuffed chair. His dappled foot dangles loosely over the edge, and one spotted ear is flapped up to reveal its pink interior. Lucie sits on the chesterfield, slides a splayed hand in an arc over a large cluster of flowers. Sighs. Rises, and slowly climbs the stairs. Stands in the doorway outside Mitchell's room.

An eggplant, maybe? Wouldn't you. Mitchell?

He opens his eyes. She sees the gleam from the moonlight. Eggplant?

She emits another deep sigh. If I were an eggplant, you'd love me the same way. I'd sit on the sill until I went soft, until I rotted, wouldn't I? Eggplant wife. Untouched. Unconsumed. You still wouldn't hunger for me, would you?

Eggplant?

Oh forget it. She swings around and away. Heads down.

You're too hungry, he shouts back suddenly, his words like thick black toast flung down the stairs.

Complete silence follows. Even the house doesn't creak. He returns, she supposes, to sleep.

When Mitchell sleeps it's as though he has pulled a plug from a wall. She thumps slowly down the rest of the stairs and back to the chesterfield. Lays her left cheek carefully over a fully blown flower. The side of her face covers the blossom.

The dog whimpers, stretches out his two front legs, yawns and hops down off the chair, meanders over and licks her foot. Then, sniffing, drawn by the salty wetness, he moves his muzzle up to her face, which he covers thoroughly with wide, wet sweeps of his tongue.

God, I long to be filled.

Pushing Spot away, she sits up. Pictures milk rushing into a large, steel bowl. Poured fast, the milk curves in a wave on the bottom, white bubbles foam and gush up the sides to the top. She sees herself reach over and drink from the brim, herself the bowl, herself the milk, and the foam.

At meal time Lucie and Mitchell masticate across from each other in the dining room, eyes lowered, spoons, knives, forks touching dishes, scraping, spreading, cutting. Hands reach, pass, lift, lower. They listen to the sound of spoons against bowls, bread knives against crusts, water and ice dropping into thick deep glasses thunk thunk thunk. When the meal is finished serviettes are replaced in their rings or thrown on top of them. Mitchell pushes his chair back, rises, and says, Thanks. Lucie's chair pushes back a few minutes later. Push stand go. Push stand go.

One day, in the middle of one of these rhythmic meals, Mitchell changes the punctuation.

This is ridiculous, he says. And he carries his plate to the kitchen and sits in his father's chair. He eats there from then on.

Lucie buys seven eggplants and lines them up from large to small on the window sill. She likes to take them down one at a time, run her hands over them, set them back like dolls in a row. How shiny you are, she croons. How smooth and fine you feel. Now. How best to consume you?

"Eggplant," says Pierre Franey in *The Sixty Minute Gourmet*, is a vegetable which has "a special character, a flavour, and texture that is like no other. It has a sort of meatiness about it and it is certainly one of the most versatile of all vegetables."

The elegance of eggplant, lovely when stuffed.
Thirsty for butter, and oil,
slippery
and wet

Insatiable thirst,
for butter, for oil
Slip into me
Slip out of me
Enter me
Feed me

JULY

Lucie picks up the two lime-green, ruffled doilies from the stereo console and turns with them in a slow spiral, sending the air around her into a gentle sworl. Decision unfolding as she goes, she gesticulates at the ceiling and walks into the kitchen. She opens the cupboard door and reaches for the compost bucket under the sink. Drops the doilies in on top of the coffee grounds.

Lucie rocks gently in the garden swing, closes her eyes and imagines her perfect garden. A riot of growth, replete with the eggplants that in real life wouldn't grow. Chicken wire thick with scarlet runner bean flowers, air rich with the smell of sweet peas. Rows of lettuce, kale, green onions. Raised boxes of sage, scallions, thyme, coriander. Wire cages supporting thick vines laden with dozens of tomatoes starting to ripen. Her love, her water, her weeding have done this. Her hands have done this. She moves through the rows slowly, and pauses at each plant, touching its leaves; she lingers on the fruit, on the tomatoes, the squash, the eggplants. I love you, she whispers. One, by one, by one.

She stops swinging, opens her eyes, and surveys her actual garden. In another month or so, it will resemble her fantasy more closely. She gazes on the bodies of her plants; sucks in pleasure from what she has done. Vegetable love. One, by one, by one.

She looks across to the mushroom shed. She has never set foot in it. Has only stood at its doorway once, inhaled and despised the musty sporous air, been repelled by the mote-filled dull light, by the rows of dirt-filled flats with their dozens of pale white children poking their heads through the earth.

But it would be cool in there. And it is Christly hot, as Mitchell would say, out here. He is gone, out working his land with the neighbours. Lucie wipes her brow. Reaches for the lemonade at her foot. The ice has melted and the drink is tepid. Her body is slick with sweat against the plastic of the swing, and she is hot beyond belief. Too hot to move.

AUGUST

Mitchell's friend Lorne, in his new blue pick-up truck. Travelling slowly for a change. To keep the dust off his new paint job. An eagle on each door. In its clutches, the eagle—purple, silver, and red—carries a naked woman—light brown and pink with long blonde hair that curls in tendrils at the ends. Lorne revs the engine before he switches it off and hops out. Spot crawls out from under the house and runs over to him. Rooom. Rooom. Slam. What does he want? Go away, Lorne.

Hi. Mitch is in town.

Huh.

He should be right back.

Wanted to show him my new paint job. Fresh out of the shop. Pretty unique, eh?

Yes. Suits you.

Lorne rubs his chin. It's a fantasy. I picked it out. The guy had a whole catalogue.

It's great.

Thanks. Well I guess I've got time for a quick beer. He winks. If you're twisting my arm.

Sure.

He sits down on the steps while she goes in to the kitchen. As she comes out the glaring sun blinds her and the screen door bounces behind her.

Garden's looking good, Lorne says as she sits down beside him. Together they look out over the vegetable leaves and the half-pulled rows of carrots, parsnips, onions.

Amazingly enough. Me and my cobalt thumb. I tried to grow cabbages but the bugs got them early. It doesn't matter. I don't like cabbage.

I like it, he says. Cabbage rolls. Coleslaw. How's the 'shrooms?

Growing, I suppose. I don't like going in there. It's depressing. Mitch looks after them. I'd rather grow flowers. I'd rather that old place were full of skylights and, I don't know, dahlias. Chrysanthemums. Something big and showy.

I like 'shrooms. Fried up. Can't fry up flowers. He winks again, this time with both eyes.

Me too. I make them with marjoram, lemon juice, olive oil, and butter. And a hint of garlic. Mmm. We eat a lot of mushrooms, she says, meeting his glance then dropping her eyes to her dirty toes, which she wiggles. He guzzles the last of his beer, and belches. Then he interlocks his fingers and crushes the can in his hands. What else can he do with those hands? she wonders idly. Good things? Shut up, she tells herself. How desperate are you?

Lorne? Did you know Mitchell's parents well?

Pretty well, I guess. Good folk. Pretty f-in' odd what happened, eh? Mitch says the cops think they're okay, though. That they'll find them.

Yes. That's what he says.

Don't get much weirder than that. My old man was friends with his old man, you know.

I know.

They sit in silence. Lucie sighs deeply. Why doesn't he

go? She matches the lines on the palm of one hand to that of the other, beginning with the segments of her fingers, ending with the lines before her wrist. If people could be so well-matched.

Lorne picks at the rough edge of his cutoffs, and Lucie watches his fingers move against his skin. The hair on his upper thigh is golden. The skin is deeply brown from working outside. Except for his hands, he sits perfectly still. At ease. His hands are loosely interlocked; his forearms rest on his knees three or four inches from her brown arms.

Something. He's emitting something and her chemicals are responding, her nipples are hard. She offers him another beer. Her breast brushes his right biceps as she gets up; her heart pounds. She stands sweating in the cold air of the refrigerator.

Need cooling off? Lorne says low, beery breath in her ear. He is standing right behind her. If Mitchell hadn't oiled those hinges she would have heard him come in. From staring directly into the light she can't see a thing. She can smell him, though, his breath and his sweat.

Oh. You're right there.

You got that right. Right here. He presses against her. Now she can feel his cock. His breath on her neck. He pushes against her. Slowly. Steadily.

Oh, she says, but doesn't move.

That all you have to say? he says. His tongue touches her ear. His hand clips her breast, her nipple.

Stop, Lorne, she says, her voice breaking.

What's the matter?

She can hardly speak. Her voice is harsh, breathless. Just quit it.

The dogs start up, and Spot appears, salivating, excited, and dusty, on the other side of the screen door. He's been out chasing cars again, bad dog. Then she hears the truck door slam.

Mitchell, she says, and moves away, heart pounding, flesh wakened, thirsty; thirsty.

Mitchell smiles a welcome to Lorne. The hand that has just felt Lucie's breast clasps Mitchell's hand. Hey, bud. The dogs in the kennel are going nuts. Cool it, Mitchell calls out loudly to them, and they do. Lorne looks him right in the eye. Smiles. How's it hanging, man?

Good. Good, says Mitchell. You? He is picking the price label off the clippers and doesn't look up. Lucie's eyes dance around the yard, bounce off post, leaf, flower, net, fly, stalk, sun.

Mitchell now looks at Lorne, then back at Lucie. Beer, Lorne?

Just got one. Thanks, bud.

Luce?

No, thank-you. Water. Water is fine.

Lucie, awash with guilt and heat, turns and enters her garden, crouches down at the beginning of a row. Draws small trenches with trembling fingers.

I must focus my thoughts. Somehow. Think and do not stop. What will quell this shaking? How I used to hate to garden, but it was part of my chores. Clipping around the patio until my hands and wrists ached. Why, Mum? Why can't the gardener do everything? The smell of the cut grass. The tough little weeds that would break before they'd pull out. They pull out here; they're deep, and easy. At home I refused to weed the pansy bed, where I'd seen the dog go pee. I can see Mum in her gardening garb digging in the earth, kneeling in the earth planting bulbs. Hands in embroidered canvas gloves. My body is humming, body hot. The men's laughter is like some smashing thing. Men. Mitchell; Lorne. Men. Oh God. Concentrate.

How much I liked to water when I was a little girl. Made moats around all the plants. Liked to stand with the hose and saturate,

make rain storms happen, make puddles for the birds to bathe. Like this. Like this. Quench thirsts of plant and animal. Help all things grow. But that was the coast; there wasn't such a need for water. Here, I could stand with the hose all day in the hot sun, and tomorrow everything would be dry. Thirst. Unslakable thirst.
Oh God I'm so empty.
Drink that water. Drench in water. Now.

Faced away from the men, away from the house, she pauses to listen to herself, still aroused, still sweating, wet, and trembling. A pulse in her throat, in the back of her knee. She can see it in the water leaving the hose. Exhilaration, fear, or both? Couldn't do it; can't do it. Guilt. Love. Pull those carrots. Yank those weeds. Garden. Mushrooms. Hell.

Hey Luce. We're going into town for supper, calls Mitch. The two men are standing by Lorne's truck. Want anything?

She goes over, hose in her hand.

Don't go. I'm cooking dinner. I'm going to make you an eggplant casserole. I had to buy the eggplants, she says to Lorne.

Want to come with us? asks Lorne.

No, I—

Well, have fun, says Mitch. Come on. And off they go. Spot chases them down the driveway.

In the bathroom she runs a sink full of cold water, bathes her face, her hands, her arms. Smiles ruefully at herself in the mirror. Poor old virtuous you, she says. Then she runs the warm, to wash. Reaches for a clean towel and knocks Mitch's shaving kit on the floor. Sees a letter. Credit cards.

Picks up the letter. Unfolds it. The letter is dated the last day of February.

Dear Mr. Patterson: We are sorry to inform you that your parents' bodies have been found. However, we are sure it is a relief to you to know, finally. . . .

Dead. Drowned. The letter asks for instructions. The credit cards are his father's. Canadian Tire. Sears.

Casserole of Lamb and Eggplant

1 large eggplant, about 1 1/2 pounds
1/4 cup olive oil
1 teaspoon finely minced garlic
1 1/2 pounds ground lamb
Salt and freshly ground pepper
1/2 teaspoon ground cinnamon
1 bay leaf
1 dried hot pepper
4 cups (1 1-pound, 12-ounce can) tomatoes with tomato paste
1 cup bread crumbs
1/2 cup grated Parmesan or Gruyère cheese

Method:
1. Preheat the oven to 425 degrees.
2. If the eggplant is not young and tender, peel it; otherwise, leave the skin intact and just trim the ends.
3. Cut the eggplant into 1-inch-thick slices lengthwise. Cut the slices into strips 1 inch wide. Cut the strips into 1-inch cubes. There should be about six cups.
4. Heat the oil in a casserole and add the onion and garlic. Cook, stirring, until the onion is wilted. Add the lamb, chopping down with the side of a heavy metal spoon to break up any lumps. Add the eggplant and cook, stirring often, about 5 minutes.
5. Add the pepper, the cinnamon, and bay leaf, the hot pepper, and tomatoes. Cook, stirring often, about 5 minutes.
6. Spoon and scrape the mixture into a casserole or baking dish. Sprinkle with a mixture of crumbs and cheese. Place in the oven and bake 15 minutes.
Yield: Four to six servings.

SEPTEMBER

Shortly after the first time she cooked for Mitchell—early on, before he moved in—they lay on their backs on her waterbed, too full to do more than groan. He'd brought lamb chops, and fresh vegetables. His mother had sent a box on the bus. After dinner, they lifted each other's shirts and compared taut belly mounds.

Over here we have the new potatoes, he said.

And over here?

The carrots, and the beans.

Thank-you, Mitchell's mother and dad, she said. Do tell them thanks from me.

You know, said Mitchell, I can picture my parents out in the garden. My dad digging the potatoes, my mum gathering the beans. I can see them so clearly.

I can hardly wait to meet them. Have you told them about your new girlfriend yet?

No. But there's plenty of time for that. You're going to be around a long time, right?

I hope so. But I'd really like to get to know your family. Even a little. Don't you think they'd like me? Is that it?

What is this? An interrogation? I guess we'll get out there to the farm one of these days. In the meantime, Lucie, I have a good idea.

Oh?

Every month or so she'd ask him again. Have you told your parents about me?

Slipped my mind, he'd say. Or, Gosh, I forgot. Next time for sure.

With the sun and her generous watering Lucie's garden has flourished and ripened over the summer, but now so much is at a standstill. Waiting. Waiting. For what? Just a few woody radishes left. A few scarlet runner beans growing wrinkled and old on their vines, their pods paling into brown. All that vegetable love. So much lovely greenness. Now to be nipped. Doomed by frost one day soon.

Lucie lifts her head, drooped and pale, looks out over the horizon. The landscape beyond her garden is flat and motionless and steady. If she looks hard enough, she can make it undulate, like the waves in the inlet when she was a little girl looking out over the ocean. Solid blue and steady stubble yellow. Until she closes her eyes. From colour to gloom to colour. To white.

Lucie sits on the bed braiding her hair, then winds the braids into circles and pins them up. From the corner of her eye she watches the curtain flutter in the window. The moussaka she made this afternoon smells warm and rich as it bakes downstairs. How many recipes she can make with eggplants! She has ironing to finish once she is done here; three newly laundered cotton dresses need pressing. In fact, they're still on the line.

Spot comes silently—except for the tick-ticking of his claws on the hardwood—into the bedroom. Reaches up and licks her under the arm. Then he climbs up on the bed, curls his plump and solid body up against her and sighs. Shifts slightly and rests his head on her lap. He watches the curtain flicker too, his ears and eyes alert. She lies back, rests her hands on her belly. She undoes the buttons on her dress; hikes up her skirt.

Listens to the gentle wind at the window, listens to the dying leaves rustle.

Imagine a woman lover, then. Imagine her soft breast against your soft breast, her smooth cheek against yours. Finding yourself in other, other in yourself, and yet, at the same time, such difference. Undulation, curve, soft flesh. There are men with soft mouths, soft skin. There are men with soft hands, smooth cheeks. But an all-

encompassing softness and pliancy. How to describe sleeping with a woman?

Let me eat guava, papaya, persimmon. Let me peel an avocado and scoop out ripe green flesh.

Let me consume sounds soft as steamed pork buns, soft as fresh, warm bread pulled from its crust.

Her body is curves and concaves. When she lies on her side, each hip is a gentle moon slice of bone. Her skin is smooth, and smells of roses.

Your land is familiar to her from her own flesh and bone. The tips of her fingers are moist with cucumber lotion, lie flat against your nipples. She fits the palms of her hands over each of your breasts, one, then the other, knows their meaning, kisses. Her fingers are tender skate blades, glide down your belly and along your thighs. Suggesting, not demanding. Open. Open. To you, to her. Both of you, open. This woman's body has glossy nails painted peach. Her fingers are long and narrow. Their colours part you, enter you, slide gently inside you.

Lady Fingers

About 18 whole lady fingers
1/2 cup sifted cake flour
2/3 cup sifted confectioner's sugar
1/3 teaspoon salt
3 eggs
1/2 teaspoon vanilla extract

Method:
Preheat oven to moderate (350 degrees)
Sift together three times the flour, half the sugar, and the salt.
Beat the egg whites until stiff and gradually
beat in the remaining sugar.
Beat the egg yolks until thick and lemon-coloured, and

*fold with the vanilla into the egg white mixture.
Sift the flour mixture, a third at a time, over the eggs and
fold in carefully
fold
carefully,
fold me carefully, in your arms
fold me
hold me against your breast
hold me
sift me
stroke me with those smooth and gentle fingers*

Lucie leaves her canning jars in the sterilizer, leaves her mounds of pared carrots and slips on her gumboots, grabs a plaid jacket from the hook. Begins the walk across the yard. She knows she will find Mitchell in the dusty gloom of the mushroom shed.

Mushrooms, she thinks. Pick with a sharp knife. Slice off at the base of their thick stems. Pick at varying stages for various things: small, for pickling; medium, to slice or sauté; large, to stuff. Note, she adds. Mushrooms have a blotter-like capacity for butter, oil, and cream.

Note further, she says aloud. Young pale mushrooms are succulent, while the older, drier mushrooms are best for sauces, as the flavour lies in the dark gills.

The door squeaks open and beams of light fall onto row upon row of dusty flats. The musty air sucks up the moisture in her breath and throat.

Mitchell? Her voice cuts through the dusty dark. His shadowy form in the white coverall hovers at the back of the shed like a giant moth. She calls him twice more and he comes toward her.

Well, this is a first, he says. Seeing you out here.

Mitchell, this can't go on.

What's that.

You know goddamn well.

Okay, we'll talk, he says, surprisingly. Maybe we should. Talk. He leans up against one of the tables. You've changed, Lucie. I don't know what it is.

Me? I haven't changed, Mitchell. You have.

You're always trying to take over. Don't think I haven't noticed. You're pushy. You want to change everything. Correction. You want *me* to change everything.

Mitchell—

You're trying to make me do stuff I don't want to do.

Mitchell, why didn't you ever tell your folks about me?

What do you mean?

Why didn't you ever tell your parents you were living with me?

He looks down. Bursts out angrily. It was terrible having to lie to them. I hated it. But how could I help it? First I leave the farm, then I take up with a city girl.

Oh, she says. I get it. So you were ashamed of me. Of my family. Well well. The lights are coming on.

She stares at the top of his bent head. She feels herself pulled taller from inside, feels her spine straighten, feels her father's pride well up in her. Wills Mitchell's face upward, wills his eyes to meet hers.

Mitchell steps forward and back, but he eventually meets her gaze. He takes off his cap and smooths his curly black hair. His hands work and fidget. In the dark he is pale as white paper.

Recipe, she thinks. Sautéed mushrooms.

2 cups medium mushrooms

1 T butter

2 T white wine

Method:

Slice clean mushrooms. Slice them very thinly with a very sharp knife. Sauté them in one tablespoon of butter. Cook until the mushrooms give up their liquid. Then cook until

this liquid evaporates.
Into thinnnnn
aiiiiir

Look, he offers finally. Maybe you need help.
Help? Her mind stills. What do you mean?
You know. Help. A doctor.
Mitchell. The stillness turns grey. A red ember forms in the centre. Whoa. Mitchell.
She can't even force a smile.
Mitchell, she says, her voice shaking. It's *you* who needs the doctor. You—now she is choking, until fury breaks the smile and gushes forth—*you* who think your goddamn *parents* are coming back after all this time are a lot crazier than I'll ever be. *You*, who talk to them as if they are in the goddamn *room* with you. And you *know* they're dead. You've known for months and months. I found the letter, Mitchell. And the credit cards. In your shaving kit.

The words cut her lips; she can taste blood. She is blind with anger, and she knows she is being cruel. And he? He stands perfectly still, though perhaps blood trickles from one ear. He says nothing, doesn't move a muscle.

You've been fixing every goddamn thing in sight except us, Mitchell, and I've had it. I quit. Got it? She walks to the door. Opens it. Steps into the light.

Still he stands there. Still he says nothing. Does nothing. She yells into the dark.

Mitch? Your parents are *dead. D-e-a-d Dead.* They don't give a flying fuck what you do to their house. And neither do I.

OCTOBER

Y ou can stand in a door frame and push your arms out sideways against the frame. Push as hard as you can. Then take a step forward. Relax your arms at your sides. They will automatically rise, as though they have become wings. Your arms will float out from your sides as though you are Roberta Bondar in space. But only for a couple of seconds. Then they start to hurt. It's the pressure and then the release of pressure that gives you those wings. That make you feel weightless. That make you feel you could float up to the ceiling, open a skylight, and keep going, up. Up. Up.

Hazel days, and eyes, and sweater.

She throws her sandals, her high heels, her dress boots, into a cardboard box. Thunk. Thunk. Thunk. She shoves the box to the back of the closet.

She lies dead centre on his parents' bed and stares at the sky out the window.

The leaves are all gone from the trembling aspen trees. Frost has bitten the garden, bitten everything. Mitchell has added insulation to the barn. He's purchased three white sweat shirts, two more pairs of white coveralls, three white turtlenecks, and three Stanfield undershirts.

The air is always cold now, and the landscape brown. Lucie stands still, and straight, breathes deeply. The air's sharp edge feels good. Mitchell's dogs are quiet. The stars are out.

Lucie has been in the barn with the dogs, their wet noses pushed into her hand. She was glad for their company. She feels dry these days, shrivelled as soup mix legumes. Longing for moisture.

Mitchell is a large, light grey shadow, even in daylight.

He is a cold egg that will crack in boiling water.

Boiled Egg

Boiling water.
Pot.
Egg.

Note:
The difference in soft-cooked, hard-cooked, and coddled eggs is more a matter of timing than method.

Chicken In A Mug

Method:
Put one heaping teaspoon of Chicken In A Mug in a cup. Fill with boiling water. Stir.

Her dusty cookbooks sigh high on the shelves. The hinges on the recipe box rust. The cream puckers. The cooking wine sours. Shallots shrivel. Gorgonzola and brie coat with thin green fuzz. There are no vegetables in the crisper except badly wilted parsley and a parsnip. Raisins turn to red dust. Half a green pepper liquifies. Lucie stares out the windows into the sky and longs for cumulonimbus clouds. But the skies remain clear, their colour a deep persevering blue.

Mitchell?

She sees him standing outside in the middle of the driveway, staring up at the sky. There's nothing in particular to see, but she knows what he is seeing. He thinks they vanished into blue, not sea; vanished, in fact, as they departed. And she supposes they may as well have.

Every few days when she looks out she sees him there again, in the same spot, neck craned the same way, peering up.

We are both getting strange, she thinks, loosening the belt on her house dress and reaching for the loaf of bread.

Toast

Method:
Put two slices of bread in toaster. Depress lever. When ready, toast will pop up of its own accord. Butter or no butter. It really doesn't matter. Consume while hot. If you can.

Mitch?

Glass of Water

Method:
Fill glass with water from the tap. Drink.

NOVEMBER

Lucie! The cry is long, drawn out. Lucie! from the porch, up the stairs. A voice sick with grief. She rushes down. Mitchell stands in the doorway. Spot's bloody body in his arms.

Hit on the road near the driveway.

Black, white, gashed with red, smashed with red in Mitchell's arms.

Help me? he says. Pleading. Lucie? Poor stupid bugger. That poor stupid bugger didn't see a damn thing coming.

Grief pours through her, fills her to the brim and she almost buckles.

Numbly she follows Mitchell out to the kennel. He lays Spot in an empty stall, and Lucie and Mitchell stand across from each other over the straw and his body. The other dogs whine and jostle across the hall, trying to see. Lucie steps over Spot's body and goes to Mitchell, puts her arms around him.

Oh Mitchell, she says.

I know, she says.

He gives nothing back. Stands hard, erect, cold.

Help me, he says in a distant voice.

Help me, she mouths against his coat.

Aloud she says, I can't.

Lucie stands beside the hole Mitchell digs with the Wreggit's small backhoe. She tosses in a rawhide bone before Mitchell fills the grave with earth and moves the machine away. Together they stamp it down.

That night a strange noise floats over to the house from the kennels. A kind of mass whining drifts through the windows and lifts Lucie from her bed and down the stairs. No barks, no yelps. A steady hum of keening. Lucie is drawn out of the house and down the concrete walk. Not one of the dogs is outside on watch. Inside, where they spend their nights, they are congregated in the shadows, all whimpering. And in there with them, face down in fresh straw, is Mitchell. His back heaves and shakes with sobs. His dogs, with their ugly, worried faces, push their noses in his hair, between shoulder and jaw, into arm pit. He does not respond to them. The dogs don't bark when she comes in, but look up with concerned eyes, half wag their trembling stubby tails. Fall silent. Expectant.

Mitch?
Mitchell—
Don't leave me, Lucie. His voice is muffled and anguished.
Mitchell—
Please, Lucie. Please. Please don't leave me.

He drags himself to his knees, and then to his feet. He stands perfectly still, distant, looking through her. The blood drains from his face, his neck, his shoulders. She can see it leaving his limbs, sinking to his boots and filling them. Blood flows over the tops of the boots and down the sides and through the straw and onto the dirt floor of the barn. Boudin noir, Lucie thinks, and goes back to the house.

Blood Sausage: Boudin Noir

Have the sausage casings ready.
Melt 2 tablespoons lard and cook gently without browning: 3/4 cup finely chopped onions
Dice into 1/2 inch cubes and half melt: 1 lb. fresh pork fat
Cool slightly and combine gently with:
1/3 cup whipping cream
2 beaten eggs
Freshly ground pepper
1/8 tsp fresh thyme
1/2 pulverized bay leaf
Mix in:
2 cups fresh pork blood

Note: Do not completely fill casings, as the mixture will swell during the poaching period. Place the sealed casings in a wire basket, and plunge them into boiling water. Avoid overcrowding. Reduce heat at once to about 200 degrees and continue cooking for about 20 minutes.

Note: Should any of the sausages rise to the surface of the simmering liquid, pierce them to release the air that might burst the skins. They might squeal, give a small scream, but pierce them anyway. To serve, split and grill them very gently.

DECEMBER

Mitchell wears cotton batting wrapped round his head. Smudged with red food dye. He is a torn presence continually leaking sadness, resentment, and hurt into the air.

The vase of Lucie's voice is now virtually covered, a fringed scarf draped over its mouth. It is strange coming and going with this minimum of words. When they do speak, the sound is muted, distant, as though she and Mitchell are whispering through west coast fog.

Do you want half this apple, Mitchell?

No. Thank-you.

One day Mitchell is wearing a bizarre look that might be a smile on his bloodless face. It is an expression so unfamiliar that she thinks for a second he's wearing a mask. He emits a kind of anaemic happiness, though; there is a strange glow to his flesh.

I'm going into town, he says.

He hasn't left the farm in weeks. Barn, kennel, house. Out to Spot's grave. The rutted paths are clearly marked. This is a departure.

When he comes back, the skin on either side of his mouth, which is trying to grin, is like rumpled tissue paper. He waves a ticket folder before he drops it on the table.

I'm going to Hawaii, he says. For Christmas. I'm going to get them. Bring them home.

Lucie pictures Mitchell ascending like a sheet of paper in a powerful updraft. Swept back and forth, up and up, until he reaches the sky. He will be up there forever, a stratus cloud, long and lean and white. Looking, and looking.

Folded white t-shirts sit on the dryer. Beside them are white Levis, white tennis shorts, white socks and briefs. A jar of zinc oxide.

The whites of Mitchell's eyes are so utterly clear. The blue of his eyes seem paler. His hands and face are almost translucent.

Christmas Plum Pudding
The Canadian Living Christmas Book
"Gloriously fragrant with sweet spices and rum-soaked fruit, this is the ultimate in traditional Christmas puddings. One bite, topped with luscious Orange Hard Sauce, is enough to recapture all the delicious memories of Christmas past."

On Christmas morning, the ten dogs run free in the yard, their red ribbons and bells lost within ten minutes. The pack of them form a big heap on the porch, panting and glad, wait eagerly for Mitchell to appear. It may be a while, she tells them through the screen. A long, long while. You may as well relax. Enjoy the view. The cabañas. Tropical punch. The sand between your toes.

The dogs whine, then lie drooling over the smells that waft through the screen. Corn bread. Bacon. Spinach timbales. Lucie has decided to be Edwardian, in a white cotton and lace nightgown. Stands barefoot in the kitchen doorway, behind the screen, hair tousled in a loosened braid. The ties at the front of her gown are undone, reveal breast bone, the gentle swell of her breasts' flesh. If she gets chilly, she will pull on an aubergine wool dressing gown. Belt it firmly. And get back to her cooking.

She makes peach waffles, broiled and spiced sausage patties, tipsy melon balls. She sets the table with a red cloth and sterling silver. She builds a roaring fire.

At the breakfast table she toasts the day. Merry Christmas. Merry Christmas. Pours choke cherry syrup over hot, butter-smothered waffles. Through the dining room windows she can see the white breath of Mitchell's dogs as they wrassle in the cold air. Suddenly the dogs stop, sense a presence in the yard. They stand stock still, ears cocked. And then they bark, jubilantly, the way they do when Mitchell comes home.

She ignores them, and spikes her coffee with Kahlua, and sits on her love seat. She peruses her new gardening books. In the spring she is going to plant Indian corn. Swiss chard, bok choy, Japanese eggplant. The second year of a garden is always better.

And she will grow more than vegetables. She will grow lilies, roses, orchids, chrysanthemums. She will grow abundance.

In the spring, I will grow chrysanthemums, she says loudly in a clear, certain voice. In the spring I will knock down the mushroom shed. Build a greenhouse.

The cool breeze turns icy. Somebody disapproves. She gets up to give the door a slam. Notices a sudden and complete stillness. Silence. She looks out the kitchen window.

Gone. The dogs have vanished. Not one yip, not one paw print or patch of yellow remain in the yard. The surface of the snow, except where Mitchell's footsteps leave the house, are virginal. She feels calm. She is good, now, at being alone.

Hearts of Palm

If you live in California, Hawaii, or Florida, you can have fresh hearts of palm. But be sure to eat them as soon as peeled, for they discolour quickly. Cut into dice, sprinkle with lemon juice, and serve with French dressing made with lime juice.
If you don't live in California, Hawaii, or Florida, cut chilled canned hearts of palm into lengthwise strips.
Serve on Romaine lettuce garnished with stuffed olive slices & green pepper rings
Sprinkle with chopped parsley & paprika
Serve with French dressing, or mayonnaise